THE KNIGHTS

OF

REDEMPTION

A NOVEL

Matt Micros

For my family and friends...

TABLE OF CONTENTS

THE KNIGHTS OF REDEMPTION

We are all Knights of Redemption. Each possessing the power to listen, learn, teach and inspire...

I.
henry whitman

What if everyone's life was judged solely by the worst thing they had ever done? World leaders would no longer be judged by a successful economy or their social programs, but rather, for inappropriate advances on underpaid interns. Professional athletes wouldn't be heroes for hitting 50 home runs or throwing 40 touchdowns in a season, but for refusing to sign an autograph for a ten year old boy in a wheelchair.

Long before he became President of one of the most prestigious universities in the country, Henry Whitman was a five year old boy who wrestled his hand from his father's grasp and chased someone two city blocks just to give the man a quarter he had dropped.

When he was ten, he set up a lemonade stand on a street corner with a sign that told customers *exactly* how much each glass had cost him to make, because he didn't want them to feel as though he was unfairly marking the prices up. When he was a senior in high school and was asked to the Sadie Hawkins Spring Fling by two girls—one of them, a sweet, but not entirely attractive oboe player in the band; the other, the captain of the cheerleading squad and a future Miss Connecticut—he went with the oboe player because she had asked him first.

And when his hard working father couldn't afford to send him to college on his factory worker's hourly wage, Henry put himself through by working two jobs and commuting from home to keep the costs down. Once he finally completed his schooling and began bringing home a steady paycheck—it took him nearly ten years to do it--he gave nearly half of it each pay period to his parents because he was grateful they had allowed him to live at home the entire time. He lived by the words of Mark Twain. *"Always do right. It will gratify some people, and astonish the rest."* In fact, it would not be a stretch to say that Henry Whitman made the correct moral and ethical decision in his life every single time-- except the one that mattered most.

Henry's first job was as a professor of English at a small, but well-known liberal arts college in Boston. His students loved his classes for he taught them not only an appreciation of literature, but also the crucial life skills of writing and communication. And he did so with an enthusiasm that couldn't possibly have been disingenuous. When they studied Mark Twain, he came to class dressed at Twain. When they studied Fitzgerald, he threw Roaring 20's parties at his house for the entire class and even a few that weren't in it. If students had a problem, whether it be socially, financially or ethically, he was the moral compass they sought out. Which is what made it that much more difficult for them when he was offered to head up the department, and his teaching load was cut in half. He was forced to teach fewer students and had less free time as well. Eventually, he was offered the equivalent position at an even more prestigious college, but when he refused to leave until his current employer had found a suitable replacement for him, he lost out on the other position.

Henry first met his wife at a coffee shop, when he eyed her reading an obscure novel by a long passed away author he admired. He was nearly 40 at the time and said he knew she would be the woman he would marry the moment she peered up at him over the book, her blue eyes looking even larger through a pair of horned rimmed reading glasses. She taught high school freshman English in Watertown, just outside of Boston, but when Henry's parents both grew ill at the same time, he and his wife moved to Connecticut to take care of them and begin a family of their own.

Both had to make sacrifices to do so. Bernadette accepted the only position available to her—a remedial teaching position at a middle school; a job that caused her to literally count down the days to each vacation and the end of the school year. Middle school students were monsters, filled with energy, hormones and a lack of filters that resulted in some of the most outrageous comments coming from their mouths. Her job was living proof that no good deed went unpunished.

Henry fared quite a bit better due to his background and was offered the position of Head of School at Choate. Five years later, he decided he missed being in the classroom and accepted a full-time professorship at nearby Yale. But even though his love was teaching, he kept getting pulled into administration and two months into the school year, he assumed the Department Chair position on an interim basis when the Chair had a stroke. A year later, Henry had the interim tag removed, three years after that, he became the Vice President of Academic Affairs, and five years after that, at age 62, he became President of the University.

He and his wife had two beautiful and well-behaved teenagers (an oxymoron if ever there was one), a nice house in the suburbs, and enough money to live comfortably, if not extravagantly. And then, as if overnight, everything came to pieces one April morning. The thing was, it didn't really happen overnight. Henry had just missed all of the signs.

The day had begun just like any other day. Henry had about a half dozen phone messages and two dozen emails to return, along with responding to three or four invites to university functions that he would need to attend. At 10:00am, he had a meeting with a distinguished alum who was interested in donating a million dollars to help fund building a soccer specific stadium on campus. At 11:30, just as he was about to head out for an early lunch, he received the call. He normally would have let his secretary answer it, but he could see she wasn't at her desk, and he also noticed it was an in-house call, so he grabbed it. Couldn't very well call himself a man of the people, if he wasn't accessible *to* the people.

"Hello," he answered as if he was answering his house phone.

There was silence on the other end of the line for a moment or two as the person was undoubtedly caught off guard. "Dr. Whitman?" a female answered at last.

"Yes," he said. "How can I help you—" he glanced at the caller ID, "Cheryl is it?"

"Yes," she said. She spoke very quietly, as if she was worried about someone overhearing her. "I was wondering if I could have a few minutes of your time. I normally wouldn't bother you, but I don't know who else to turn to. It's really important."

Henry glanced at his watch, and seemed to be turning over in his mind the effect that an unscheduled meeting would have on the rest of his day, before relenting. "Sure, Cheryl. Come on up. You know where my office is?"

"Yes, I do. Thank you."

Five minutes later, his intercom buzzed. "A Cheryl Rueben is here to see you," his secretary said. "She says you're expecting her?"

"That's right. Send her in."

Cheryl worked for Don Peterson in the fundraising office, working primarily on the Annual Fund. She was young—late twenties maybe—and more sexy than pretty, with a slightly worn appearance the result of living a hard life in her teens. She had worked at Yale for slightly more than three years, but he didn't know much about her other than what he overheard from others. She was a single mother of two little girls to two different fathers, neither of whom she had married. She actually came from old money in Long Island, and had lived a wild life probably in an attempt to rebel against her family as much as anything. Cheryl had attended nearby Poquonic College, known for being a country club type refuge for the tri-state area student who didn't want an education to interfere with their social life. After graduation, she worked as an intern in the development office at Poquonic for a few years, before coming to Yale. How she landed her current position was a mystery to most, but she did her job, and Henry hadn't received any complaints about her, so he didn't ask many questions. He trusted that Don knew what he was doing, as evidenced by an ever-burgeoning endowment.

"What can I do for you, Cheryl?" Henry asked curiously. Rarely did he allow himself to take a meeting without being properly prepared first.

"I'm not sure how to begin," she stammered, a bit overwhelmed now that she found herself face to face with the most powerful man in arguably the most powerful university in the country.

"Begin by just telling me what's on your mind."

She paused for a moment before beginning. "I was really excited when I got this job. I meet interesting people every day. I get to go to great events..."

"But..."

"I'm being harassed by Don Peterson," she blurted out at last.

"What do you mean by harassed? Yelled at for your work?"

"Sexually harassed."

"By Don?" he asked incredulously.

"It started shortly after I started working for him. Emails at first, telling me what to wear to department meetings. Low-cut tops, short skirts, stiletto heels. I thought he was joking, but then he started refusing to sign off on my vacation days, even though I had some coming. Eventually, he started calling me late at night, saying sexually explicit things and demanding phone sex, so he could—this is really uncomfortable for me," she said, stopping herself short.

"I don't mean this to sound insensitive, but did you in any way, even inadvertently, give him any indication it was reciprocal? Don't get me wrong. He's married and it would still be wrong, but I'm just trying to understand it because it sounds so out of character for the Don I know."

She thought about it for a moment before answering. "I've wondered that same thing for a long time, but the answer is no. I would tell him I was going to sleep. I even stopped answering the phone."

"And did it stop?"

"It got worse. He would berate me in front of the others. Then he started demanding oral sex or he'd fire me."

"When?! Where?!"

"In his office. He'd lock the door and close the blinds. But everyone knew what was going on. It was mortifying." She was crying now.

"That was my next question. Who else knows about this?"

"The other men in the office," she sniffled. "Because he told them they could run the train on me."

"I don't know what that means," Henry said.

"One of them would have sex with me from behind, while I was forced to give oral sex to the other."

The immortal words of Gary Coleman in *Different Strokes* came immediately to mind. *"Whatchu talkin bout Willis?"* Henry had lived a pretty sheltered life, and this was an area he had very little experience in. He was mortified, but decided to try and stick just with the facts.

"Do you have any emails or texts from him?" he asked.

"He makes me delete them all. He stands right over me while I do it."

"I see."

She was sensing that he didn't believe her. "I know this is all pretty difficult to believe. But it's true. Every word of it. And the only reason I didn't come forward sooner is because I really need this job. I'm a single mother, trying to raise two kids. My parents cut me off long ago when I made some poor decisions."

"Is there anyone else who can corroborate your story? Anyone at all?"

"There are others. They've never said anything to me, but I can tell."

"How can you tell?"

"Because they have the same look on their face that I see every time I look in the mirror."

"Do you think any of them would speak up?"

"I doubt it."

Henry walked across the room. Poured himself a glass of Scotch. It was a little early in the day, but if ever there was something that warranted it, this was it. "You do realize without any proof or any other people backing up your story, it will be difficult to do anything about this."

"I know, but I had to say something."

"I'll look into this," Henry promised. "But understand, as soon as I do, you could get some pushback. And I can't do anything about that without proof. So what I'd do in the meantime, is get some proof."

Cheryl nodded a disappointed nod and let herself out.

The moment she left his office, a hundred thoughts competed for a place within his mind. On one hand, Don Peterson appeared to be a family man. Married for more than twenty years with three children, he coached his son's little league baseball team and his wife was by his side for every Yale function. On the other, was that Henry had always found him to be a bit of a slickster—part corporate executive fundraiser, part used car salesman, complete with the jet black, slicked back hair. Another red flag should have been the turnover within his department since taking over five years ago. When he began the job, he had seven men and three women working under him, with an average age of somewhere in the vicinity of fifty years old. Now there were seven *women,* all extremely attractive, and just three men working there with an average age that couldn't have been even thirty. Henry had chalked it up to a natural turnover that occurred whenever you had an older staff to begin with, plus his new staff had been extremely successful. The Yale endowment had never been higher.

He decided to meet individually with the other members of the department to see what they knew, but if they knew anything, they weren't saying.

Don himself simply stated, "She's just pissed because I refused her vacation time two days before our big gala dinner dance because there was a ton of work that needed to be done. As you know, it's the biggest event of the year and we needed all hands on deck. She wanted to go to Cabo with a few of her friends. Anyway, she's been pissed off ever since."

It sounded plausible. Don had a way of making anything seem plausible. Which was probably also why he was so good at his job.

"Do you recall ever saying anything that she could have misconstrued as being sexual in nature?"

"Absolutely not."

"What about telling her what to wear into the

office?"

"If anything, I tell them all to tone it down a bit. Some of them, her in particular, tend to dress like they're going clubbing."

Still not completely satisfied, Henry sought out someone in the computer technology department. Stephen Schuler had worked there for a little over three months, but had quickly gained Henry's trust. He was sharp, reliable and discreet.

"Schu, is it possible to retrieve someone's work email even if it's been deleted?" Henry asked.

"Yes, but I'd need the actual computer to do it."

Since Don always took his laptop home with him at the end of a day, anything that was going to be done needed to be done *during* the day. While Henry took Don to lunch one afternoon, Schuler cloned Don's computer and swapped it out with the original, so he could have enough time to thoroughly search the hard drive. Don would be none the wiser.

Two days later, Schu walked into Henry's office with a memory stick. "You're not going to like what I found," he said.

On the stick were hundreds of emails, mostly graphic in nature, covering not only what to wear to work, but how nice certain body parts of hers looked. And they weren't just to her, but to several, if not all of the other female members of the office as well. It was more of a smoking gun than OJ racing down the 405 Freeway in his Ford Bronco.

It left Henry with four choices to choose from.

Ignore it, and hope the girl eventually quit. With no evidence to support her claims, she would have a difficult time proving anything. But heaven forbid she could...

He could offer to buy her silence by paying her off with a confidentiality clause that would prevent her from talking about it to anyone. Since she needed the money, this was an appealing option, although getting approval from the Board of Directors without a proper explanation, might be a bit tricky.

He could fire Don on the spot. But that would likely result in a very ugly, very public mess that the media would pounce on. The statement that "there's no such thing as bad publicity" did not apply to institutions of higher learning.

He could force Don into an early retirement. That wouldn't be easy to do since Don was only 51, but looking at a nice severance package, and a reference for future employment while staring at a memory card full of evidence, might be enough to coerce him to go away quietly. But if it wasn't, things could get ugly.

"What do you want me to do, Dr. Whitman?" Schuler asked.

"Is this the only copy?" was Henry's response.

"Yes."

"Well, I guess there's only one thing *to* do. I'll take care of it, Schu. Thanks."

Henry sat motionless at his desk after Schuler left, holding the memory stick in front of him with both hands for five or ten seconds, before snapping it in two and throwing it into the garbage.

That night as he and his wife prepared for bed, his doorbell rang. Henry answered it in his bathrobe and was greeted by two uniformed police officers. "Can I help you?" he asked.

"Dr. Whitman?" one of the officers asked.

"Yes?"

"We have a warrant for your arrest."

II.

rogers conner

Rogers Conner was named Sports Illustrated's "Athlete of the Year" after smashing 52 home runs and coming within one out of leading the Chicago Cubs to their first World Series title since 1908. He was a twenty-six year old rookie. Down 5-2 in the bottom of the 8th inning, he hammered a 2-2 fastball deep into the Chicago night, sending Wrigley Field's fans into a frenzy.

The Grand Slam, his history making 6th home run of the series, gave the Cubs a 6-5 lead heading into the ninth inning. But when their normally reliable closer let the game slip away, and his teammates couldn't rally in the home half of the inning, it was just another horrific ending for a franchise that had suffered no shortage of them over the years. It was the irony of ironies that Rogers had been named after a Hall of Famer who had played for the Cubs biggest rival, the St. Louis Cardinals. Luckily his father never lived to see him suit up for the Cubs.

Back when he was a five foot nine inch, one hundred-sixty-five pound high school center fielder in Redding, Connecticut, that had more bunt singles than home runs, Rogers had always exhibited the epitome of sportsmanship and even a modicum of modesty. It was in large part due to the influence of his father. A competitive athlete in his day, he lived by the rule that you played hard, but when it was over, you shook hands and exhibited the same sportsmanship in losing that you would if you won. Rogers found at an early age that piano lessons instead of baseball were more of a promise than a threat. He had once made the mistake of leaving the field after losing a game without shaking his opponents hands, and he found himself playing Chopsticks and Heart and Soul for the next month before he was allowed to pick up a baseball bat again.

But two things happened over the summer following his junior year that changed his life forever. The first was that he grew six inches. The second was that he lost his father to a heart attack. The first gave him a long, loping swing that enabled him to reach pitches he could only previously wave at. The second resulted in a glaring lack of discipline and sportsmanship when confronted with his newfound success. His mother was a wonderful person. She was just tired and scared at the prospect of having to raise two kids by herself, along with the financial responsibilities that came along with it, on her teaching salary of forty thousand dollars a year.

Rogers's only way to college was through a scholarship, so he spent nearly every free moment working out and working on his fundamentals. The result was fifty additional pounds of muscle mass, and a .434 batting average with twelve home runs his senior year. The problem was, by the time that happened, there wasn't much scholarship money still available. But when a player who had committed to USC, decided to sign with the Orioles minor league system instead, it opened up a scholarship at the last minute. Not to mention, USC's assistant coach had been a childhood friend of Rogers' American Legion coach.

About the same time, he received a phone call telling him the Cubs had drafted him in the amateur draft despite being told he was heading to college. With money tight, even with a full scholarship in hand, Rogers surprised everyone and signed a pro contract with a $200,000 signing bonus. He spent three years at Class A ball, as he tried to make the adjustment to four pitch pitchers, instead of the part-time ones he had faced in high school who just heaved the ball as hard as they could when they weren't playing in the outfield. He eventually made it to Triple A on his power hitting potential alone, but twenty-three year olds who had already spent five years in the minors and hadn't yet had a "cup of coffee" in the majors were labeled as career minor leaguers.

Three years later, injuries and rain outs forced the big league club to play five games in three days to wrap up the season, and as one of only two first basemen still healthy on their forty man roster, Rogers was finally called up from Des Moines, Iowa and summoned to Chicago. He arrived at Wrigley an hour before first pitch and saw that his name had been penciled into the lineup card in the 5th spot. There were using the game as a throw away against the league's top pitcher, and sat four regulars. The Cubs lineup was a Who's Who of nobodys and never will bes; or so they thought, until Rogers smashed the first pitch he ever saw in the majors, over the left field wall. Two additional home runs later, and Rogers Conner became the first player in Major League history to hit home runs in his first three at bats. He never returned to Iowa.

The following spring, in his first full season in the majors, he led the Cubs to the World Series. In the days that followed, however, after very publicly blasting his teammates in the media, he quickly became persona non grata in Chicago. His accomplishments were met with tepid acceptance, while his failures were met with boos and catcalls. Eventually, when his accomplishments began to far outweigh his failures, and he learned to keep his mouth shut when things didn't go his way, he gained a broader fan base—and a new contract worth $172 million dollars for eight years. But as he approached his mid-30's, and his numbers began to decline, the Cubs decided to let him walk for the final years of his career, rather than get into a bidding war with the Yankees, Phillies and the Los Angeles Dodgers.

After years of feeling like he was always arriving a day late for the prom, Rogers felt as though he was finally in demand, and successful. He had fame. He had fortune. He had no shortage of women after him. In fact, he was successful in every manner except the one that would have mattered to Thomas

Conner most. He was despised. Literally. He was voted the "Player You Would Least Like to Play With" by an anonymous straw poll of players done by Sports Illustrated.

It wasn't any one thing he did that made him unpopular, but rather every thing he did. He stopped speaking to reporters following the World Series because he felt he was misquoted. He never went over to congratulate a teammate for a big hit, pitch or play in the field. He rarely signed autographs, reasoning that the ones he did sign for people would be worth more. He kept to himself in the locker room, sat by himself on the plane and ate alone on the road. If he went out, it was usually with equally self-loathing, disguised as arrogance, Hollywood types. He wasn't married, but he had been dating the same woman with whom he shared a child he didn't see much, for the past eight years. But the relationship could hardly be classified as monogamous with his weakness for cocktail waitresses that spanned more than twelve major league cities throughout the country.

And yet, amazingly, Rogers found himself oblivious to the way others perceived him, until one fateful April day made it impossible to ignore any longer. He was in New York to sign with the Yankees and decided to take in a Knicks game at night. Seated courtside at Madison Square Garden in between Kevin Costner and Eva Longoria, his face suddenly appeared on the giant Jumbotron above the court, but what he expected would be a raucous ovation from fans he thought were desperately excited to see him swing the lumber in a few short days, could have been more accurately described as indifference at best, and a hailstorm of negativity at worst, with catcalls raining down from the blue seats in every direction. It was noticeable enough that he bid Kevin and Eva a hasty farewell and went into the private Delta Club for a beer.

It was largely empty at this point with the game going on, save for a woman who slid up next to him at the bar. Her face wasn't exactly that of a bulldog chewing a wasp, but she was certainly more sexy than pretty, with curves in all the correct places that were accentuated by the form fitting blue dress she was wearing.

"Didn't like the fans reaction, huh?" she said.

"Stupid New Yorkers," he said, not even looking up.

"I agree with you. But you know, you are kind of an asshole."

Normally that type of comment would result in Rogers cursing at the person and walking away, but he was intrigued by this woman for some reason. That and he sensed it wouldn't bother her much if he did.

"Now, how do you know that? We just met."

"I read the papers. I've also seen you blow past your share of kids looking for a high five or autograph," she answered.

"What are you? A stalker or something?" he asked. He had met his share of those.

"No," she laughed. "I used to date the Assistant General Manager for the Phillies, so I get to a lot of games."

"So that's it. You wanted me to play for the Phillies."

"Oh, I could have cared less where you decided to play. He and I broke up ages ago. I just thought you were hot and you looked like you needed a friend."

"I've had lots of friends. They didn't take," he said before taking another generous swig of his beer.

"In that case, friendship's overrated. I just think you're hot."

Rogers looked her over from head to toe. "You want to go somewhere?"

"Where?" she asked.

"I have access to a suite here at the Garden," he responded.

She raised her eyebrow, knowing exactly what he meant.

"Lead the way, bat boy," she said with a seductive smile.

They had made it about five feet inside the room before Rogers shamelessly had her dress halfway over her head. He was having his way with her, an attractive but far from beautiful complete stranger, for no other reason than he could. Five minutes after he had given her what he thought was probably the best thirty seconds of her life, the door to the room was thrown open and two NYPD detectives entered along with arena security.

"Rogers Conner," one of the detectives began, "You're under arrest."

"Under arrest?" he responded defiantly as he pulled on his pants. "For what?!"

"For solicitation of sex."

He spun around to face the woman in question. "You're a prostitute???"

She shrugged. "Did you think I slept with you because you were cute?"

"Umm, it has happened before," Rogers said.

"Well, not this time, sport," the other officer said.

"I didn't offer to pay her anything!"

"Guess we'll just have to sort this out down at the station. "Mr. Conner, please place your hands behind your back."

As they read him his rights, a loud cheer could be heard inside the arena, as the Knicks took the lead. The only cheer that might have rivaled it, would have been if the sight of Rogers in handcuffs had been shown on the Jumbotron, as he was being escorted from the Garden.

III.

hector rodriguez

Hector Rodriguez's greatest asset was also the same one that led to his downfall. Parceled out in moderate doses, loyalty was a tremendous quality, but when followed blindly, it often resulted in disaster.

Born in Juarez, Mexico long before it became known as the "Murder Capital of the World" and the "City of Death"; it used to be a place where hard working people could make an honest living. As a teenager, he worked in his father's junkyard, although his father would dispute the term "work". Hector used to set up games of baseball with neighborhood kids, using the chain link fence that surrounded the yard as their outfield wall while listening on the radio to Los Angeles Dodger games so they could hear how their hero, Dodger pitcher, Fernando Valenzuela was doing. Every now and then, they would sneak into a bar so they could watch the games on television.

Hector was a pretty fierce pitcher in his own right, mimicking Valenzuela's delivery right down to the "eye to the sky". But he was an even better hitter, possessing awesome power that made the left field wall at his father's junkyard tremble. There was talk that he could be the next great export, but life threw him a couple of curve balls along the way that prevented that from happening.

The first was his father dying from an overworked heart, while trying to provide for his family. Eighty-hour work weeks will do that to you, especially eighty hour weeks that involved heavy lifting in extreme temperatures and the uncertainty of when his next sale would come. Hector took over the family business when he was just 18 years old, working in the junkyard by day, while enrolling in college part time at night in legal studies. Ten years later, after numerous classes, an internship and a thesis, he was a lawyer, with a focus on business law. He sold the junkyard, and his law practice soared with the aid of the contacts he had made from running the family business. He became the lawyer for the people—the downtrodden who otherwise couldn't afford one—and made a good living at it. It was more the volume than anything. He needed to work 20 cases to make the same amount of money another lawyer could make in five. But he didn't complain because he felt as though he was making a difference. He also supplemented his income by taking on cases involving foreigners who had gotten themselves into trouble in Mexico. They paid well, and allowed him to take on more of the other cases.

There was one case, however, that would change his life forever. Juan Diaz had been a longtime family friend who ran a cantina in town. It was a favorite hangout of the locals, until one of the drug cartels began throwing their weight behind another establishment. It was barely noticeable at first. Only a few customers a week short. But when some of the regulars stopped coming in with no explanation, Juan knew he needed to do something. He ended up selling his soul to the devil.

The problem with associating himself with one of the cartels was that while he was making more money than before, he had to look the other way on back room drug deals, even though he was the one most exposed to the Federales. Even worse was that he could never retire. He was safe only as long as he was involved in the business. Anyone who tried to leave, would soon be executed out of fear they would turn on them. He had ignored all of Hector's prior warnings, but now needed his help after the Federales raided his place and arrested everyone inside.

Hector had been smart enough to steer clear of the cartels while practicing law. He had neither worked for nor against them over the years. But Juan getting arrested, changed all that. Hector took the case and not long after, was awakened in the middle of the night to screams from his daughter's room. Two men were sending a message. They should have perhaps found a different way to deliver it. The sight of these men pinning his wife and daughter to the ground, sent Hector into a rage that surprised even him. He entered the room with a shotgun pointed at the man on his eight year old daughter. Hector didn't hesitate. He blew the man to pieces. Before the other one could reach his gun, he met a similar fate. There was something about adrenalin that enabled a man to think clearer than he had ever thought before. Hector knew he had done exactly what needed to be done, and began the process of doing what then needed to be done as a result. He packed a couple of suitcases, and ushered his wife and daughter across the border into the United States in the middle of the night. They continued heading north until he felt they were safely out of reach of the Mexican cartel, before settling in a small town in Connecticut.

He left behind a good job, all of their money— except the few thousand dollars he had stashed under a mattress in the house--and most of their family. Hector and his family had to completely start over, but at least they were alive.

Ten years later, Hector was barely scraping by as the Assistant Manager at a car wash, living with his wife and daughter in a small apartment in a not very nice area of town, when one night, out of nowhere, two police officers showed up at his door.

IV.
matt o'malley

Matt O'Malley was that person who was good at a number of things, but not the best at anything. He was a good baseball player, but not the star. He was a good student, but nowhere near the best. He was good looking, but not the guy every girl decided they wanted to be with the second he walked into a room. All the more frustrating for him was the fact that he had been given every opportunity to succeed in life by his parents. They sent him to the best schools, introduced him to the best people, tried to build up his confidence every chance they had.

Matt was kind, loyal and generous to a fault, which put him ahead of 99% of the people on earth, not that he considered that to be any great accomplishment. He had always been taught that those were the minimum qualities that were to be expected from people.

After spending ten years on Wall Street, he decided he wanted to do more with his life than make money. He returned to Connecticut, where he studied for his Doctorate at Yale, before using said degree to become the Superintendent of an inner city school district twenty minutes from where he lived.   Teaching salaries, test scores and college placement all increased under his watch, but they came at a cost.   It was the same in every town. Those that no longer had kids in the schools, didn't want to pay for those that did.

He lived in a young town, where young families outnumbered those without children or whose children were grown, so the budget continually passed.   His success there helped him win the election for Mayor, and yet ironically, the same reasons he had success initially, were the same reasons that led to his unsuccessful run for Governor. It was at that point that Matt learned the first rule of politics. It wasn't so much a matter of doing what was right, as it was doing what was right for those that were likely to vote.

Although the county he lived in was largely Republican, the state overall was a blue state. Matt walked the fine line between both parties, not because he thought it would help him win, but because he believed no one should follow a platform. They should follow issues. And some issues fell on one side of the fence, while some fell on the other. What happened was that he ended up pissing off people on *both* sides and found himself on the receiving end of a resounding and crushing defeat that would have made Walter Mondale wince.

What followed was a downward spiral of financial troubles from having spent too much of his own money on his campaign, topped off by a wife that made little effort to hide the fact that she: A) no longer believed in him and B) was sleeping around.

He finally decided to do something about the latter, by paying the man his wife was sleeping with a visit. The same man who had been his campaign manager.

Charlie Peters was undressing in the closet of his home when Matt entered the bedroom. It was obvious from the expression on Charlie's face that he seemed resigned to the fact that this day would inevitably come. His wife, reading a book in her nightgown on the bed, let out a frightened scream.

"Sorry to startle you, Karen. I'm actually here to see Charlie," Matt said. Even in his agitated state, he hated the thought of scaring an innocent bystander, especially one he knew.

"How the hell did you get in here?!" Charlie asked, equal parts embarrassed and frightened.

"With my wife's key," Matt explained. "You know, the one you gave her so you could fuck her while *your* wife was at work."

"I have no idea what you're talking about."

"No? Well, let me refresh your memory." Matt began reading a text message from the phone in his hand, "Thank you for the key. Now I can make sure I'm good and naked by the time you get home for lunch. And by lunch I mean..." he said as he tossed the phone to Charlie's wife on the bed. "You can read it yourself."

She caught it, uncertain what to make of it or exactly how she should act.

"Don't believe him, babe. Matt's obviously under a lot of stress."

"It's his phone number. And my wife's

phone," Matt added before turning back to Charlie. "So here's how it's going to play out. You're going to jump out your window right now."

"You're out of your mind. We're three floors up. I'd break my legs. *If* I was lucky."

"Well, that's a chance I'm willing to take. And one you *should* take, because if you don't, I'm going to break them both for certain with this baseball bat."

Matt swung a short compact baseball hitter's swing and smashed a lamp to smithereens in order to emphasize his point. Charlie edged toward the window.

"Open it. And climb in."

For a split second, he seemed to be weighing his options. Charge Matt, who was a decent-sized, athletic looking guy with a bat; or jump. Matt doubled him over with a solid swing to his gut.

"Next swing is at your kneecaps," he warned.

Charlie climbed into the windowsill. He glanced at his wife for help, but she wasn't offering any.

"Make sure you roll when you hit the ground," Matt offered.

He gave him a kick-start. Then looked down from the window as Charlie proceeded to roll around the ground in agony.

Six police cars surrounded Matt's car at a stop sign a few minutes later, dragged him from the car, and shoved his face into the pavement. In retrospect, he decided there might have been a better way to handle things, as he spit out a few pieces of gravel onto the street.

V.

mo falls

Mo Falls was raised in the theatres of Broadway to thespian parents. They had both won multiple Tony Awards by the time he was five, and his extended family included nearly every actor his parents ever worked with. He was homeschooled more or less in the back stages of the theatre by a private tutor, until his parents sent him to refine his craft at the Eugene O'Neill Theatre Institute in southeastern Connecticut when he turned 16.

It wasn't long, however, before Mo decided live acting wasn't for him. He hated the idea of doing the same performance two or three hundred times and trying to make it fresh for each audience. He much preferred television and film, where he performed each scene five to ten times max, before moving onto the next project. After a run in with the Mexican Federales in Tijuana, Broadway decided he wasn't for it either. So when a family friend and star of the silver screen cast him in his next film, Mo moved to Los Angeles.

He was an instant star, combining the bad boy good looks and penetrating stare with an impeccable comedic timing that he was born with. He was also one of the handful of African American actors who had crossover appeal. Neither race nor gender nor economic status seemed to matter where Mo was concerned. Everyone loved him equally. After a few co-starring roles in big budget comedies, Mo was offered the lead in a sitcom produced by a television legend. Ten years and literally a hundred million dollars later, Mo was set for life as the star of the most popular show on TV. What homeschooling hadn't taught him, however, was how to handle success. He had never had to deal with sudden popularity in high school or college, because he hadn't attended either, and he found it quite daunting. When media outlets reported he had thrown away his millions on strippers and blow, they were exaggerating slightly. After all, he still maintained homes in the Amalfi Coast, Bermuda, and Malibu, along with a penthouse apartment above the Waldorf-Astoria in New York—in addition to a dozen cars and a private jet.

But the facts were that he drank too much, partied too frequently, and was starting to look much older than his 35 years. He didn't disagree with any of the comments about him. He simply didn't see anything wrong with them. But when the show's producer suspended production so that Mo could *dry out*, it signaled the beginning of the end for his career. He had a very public split from the show and was considered poison to work with.

So what did a multi-millionaire with a drinking and drug problem, and a penchant for expensive strippers and call girls do for an encore? He went on vacation naturally. But when his jet ended up with mechanical difficulties, for the first time in years, Mo was forced to fly commercial.

Sporting a leather jacket with a black undershirt, a Rolex, Armani shoes, and a Tiger Woods Nike baseball cap with sunglasses resting on the brim, he decided to buy everyone in the Airspace Lounge in the Jet Blue Terminal at JFK Airport a round of drinks.

The man seated next to him at the bar laughed, "It's only nine in the morning, Mo!"

"I know it's a little late to get started, but we'll just have to make up for it," Mo responded.

"What are you going to do next in your career?" the man asked. The guy was in his late-40's, probably a traveling salesman, whose closest previous brush with celebrity was using the urinal next to the kid from the *Life Cereal* commercials in the 80's.

"Whatever I want." Something would come along.

It always had.

"Anything look good?"

"This shot sure does," Mo said, downing it. "Another?"

Before the man could answer, two officers approached them.

"Mr. Falls? We need a word," the older of the two officers said in a monotone voice.

"Can it wait until we do one more shot?" Mo asked. "I hate to be sober in the morning."

"I'm afraid it can't."

The officers took him away in a golf cart as picture flashes from nearby photographers rapidly went off. Mo didn't seem terribly bothered. It wasn't the first time he had been arrested, and he doubted it would be the last. There was a reason he had his attorney on speed dial.

VI.
the breakfast club

The jail was nicer than any other he had been in. It wasn't what one would describe as lavish, but it was clean and somewhat bright. Mo was just puzzled at how long it had taken to get there.

"I hope I get my own cell," he said to the guard.

"This isn't the Waldorf Towers," the guard responded as he led him down a long corridor to a large holding cell at the end of the hall. Four men were already inside. Rogers Conner looked annoyed that he was there at all. Hector sat slumped over on the bench he was sitting on, wondering how he was going to get out of his mess, and if he couldn't, what would happen to his wife and daughter. Henry was isolated in the corner, looking despondent, while Matt seemed somewhat at peace with his surroundings. He figured he deserved to be there, and it was at least a reprieve from the seemingly never-ending newspaper stories analyzing his crushing defeat and crumbling political career.

The prison guard held the cell door open for Mo and didn't seem the slightest bit impressed to have a professional baseball player and movie star in the same cell.

"What's this? A 'My Three Sons' remake starring Chico and the Man?" Mo clamored.

The guard slid the door shut until it made a loud vault-like locking sound behind him.

"Mo Falls! I'm a big fan," Matt exclaimed.

"Of course you are. I'm funny and I'm talented," Mo responded.

"Talented and unemployed," Hector interjected surprisingly.

"What's that Chico?"

"I *said*, talented and unemployed," Hector repeated.

"That was by choice."

"Yes, they *chose* not to renew your contract."

"Because I *chose* to tell my boss he was a demonic asshole."

"Good move," Hector said, shaking his head.

"Relax. I make more money in residuals in a week than all of you combined will make in a year," Mo reasoned.

"I make 21 million," Rogers offered.

"Ok, so maybe not you. But the rest of you," Mo said before suddenly recognizing Rogers, "Holy shit! My MAN!"

He grabbed Rogers hand and pulled him close for a shoulder bump.

"Last time I saw you we were doing blow off Miss April's ass in Hef's bedroom."

"Um, that wasn't me," Rogers answered.

"It wasn't? Maybe it was Ryan Rogers. You

guys all look alike."

"So how'd you end up here, Mo?" Matt asked. He was a true fan.

"They found a couple of dime bags in my luggage," Mo answered matter-of-factly.

"Why would you bring that to an airport?!" Rogers asked incredulously.

"I have my own plane, but it was having some mechanical problems, so I had to fly commercial. I could have sworn I took all my pot out of my bag. But I was pretty wasted, so who knows? Anyway, one minute I'm doing shots in the VIP lounge waiting for my flight to the Amalfi Coast, and the next I'm being shoved in the back of a cruiser, where I passed out until I ended up here. Wherever here is."

"New Haven," Matt answered.

"New Haven?"

"Connecticut."

"I know where New Haven is," Mo exclaimed. "But why the hell did they bring me here?! I was at JFK."

"I was at Madison Square Garden," Rogers offered.

"And what did they say was the reason they brought you here?" Matt asked.

"Something about midtown jails being full."

"But there's at least three other jails between Manhattan and here."

Rogers shrugged.

"Guess there was a brawl at a nightclub in Stamford. Said I'd be better off here."

"So big fella, what'd you do? Roid rage?" Mo asked with his plentiful tactfulness.

"It was a misunderstanding," Rogers answered defensively.

"Of course it was," Mo baited.

"I signed with the Yankees this off season and I was taking in a Knicks game. I met this girl in the Delta Club during the game. She was...sexy, in a dirty sort of way--"

"I love that!" Mo exclaimed.

Rogers nodded in agreement before continuing, "So, I take her up to my suite at the Garden and I had her dress up over her head, when the cops busted in..."

"Nice!" Mo said. He was genuinely happy to hear there were other people as decadent as he was.

"Not nice. It's going to end up all over the papers in the morning. I had no idea she was a pro."

"Don't worry about it. There's no such thing as bad publicity."

"Maybe not in television. But there is in the sports world."

Mo shrugged and turned to Hector. "What about you, Chico? What'd you steal to end up in here?"

"What makes you think I stole something?" Hector said defiantly. He was clearly offended. "And the name is Hector."

"Well, you either stole something or you ran over someone's foot with a John Deere."

"I don't cut lawns for a living. Nice stereotype."

"Relax. You could work at a car wash too I suppose."

"That's a bit rascist, Mo," Matt interjected.

"Ok. Ok. So what *do* you do?" Mo continued.

Hector didn't really want to answer him. "I manage a car wash," he whispered.

Mo burst into laughter. "Seriously??? I was just playin.'"

He continued laughing until he started to cough from laughing so hard. The others tried to stifle their laughter, but even they found it ironic.

"I'm actually a lawyer," Hector added.

"Then I'd say you're a bit overqualified for your job," Mo continued, still choking on the last remnants of laughter.

"I'm not a lawyer here. I was back in Mexico."

"I got arrested down in Mexico once. Kept my ass locked up for three months," Mo said.

"So how'd you end up here, Hector?" Matt asked.

"It's a long story. But the short version is that I wanted to get my daughter out of the public school system. Two kids got stabbed in the parking lot last week and a girl got raped. They don't have enough books in the classrooms. And the teachers have to teach to the majority, which means the brighter kids don't get pushed," Hector explained.

"They don't offer any honors classes?"

"Very few, because no one wants to teach there."

"So you wanted to get her to private school."

"But I didn't have the money. Anyway, at the car wash, we have this monthly plan where people pay by credit card and can come as often as they like. I opened up a business account and took a bunch of credit card numbers and ran them through for the amount they pay at the car wash."

"That can't be more than $50 each," Rogers reasoned.

"$49.95," Hector explained, "But when you have 250 of them, that's a year's tuition."

"So you stole," Mo said.

"I *borrowed*. Figured it would take most people a couple of months to notice. At that point, the car wash would credit them, and I would pay the car wash back each week until it was covered. They would never know the difference."

"Except they did," Rogers added.

"That you stole," Mo continued.

"I intended to pay it back. Every last penny," Hector said defensively, knowing they didn't believe him.

"Technically, in order to borrow, you need to ask permission first. When you do what you and my manager did, it's called stealing," Mo said.

"I guess," Hector admitted at last.

"I'm just messing with you, Chico. Sounds like a pretty good plan." Mo turned to Matt. "How bout you GQ Hoodlum?"

"I beg your pardon?" Matt asked.

"Polo knit hat. Abercrombie hoodie. Banana jeans. You either tried to rob a bank with a paint gun, or you joined P Diddy's entourage."

"Neither actually. I'm a politician," Matt said.

"Where? You don't look very familiar to me," Mo asked.

"That's because I wasn't successful," Matt explained. "I used to be a hedge fund guy, but decided I was fed up with the current political system. I was a mayor in a small town before deciding to run for Governor as an Independent. Burned through a lot of my savings about halfway through and just rode it out to a resounding and somewhat embarrassing defeat."

"How'd you end up in here?" Rogers asked. "You steal some money as well?"

"Not exactly. It's a bit more embarrassing than that."

"It appears as though we've got nothing but time," Mo said, sitting for the first time.

"My wife was screwing my campaign manager so I smashed him with a baseball bat and kicked him out a third floor window while his wife looked on."

"How'd you find out?" Rogers asked.

"I was talking to her last week while she was driving and I kept hearing the text message beep go off. Twenty minutes later, I get a call from the police saying she had been in an accident. When I got to the hospital, they handed me her personals, her phone being one of them. It kept beeping, so I checked it and found a bunch of texts."

"That's a shitty way to find out. Did your wife die?"

"No, she's fine. Broke her leg is all. The two of them can have wheel chair races together."

"*That...*is fucking *awesome*," Mo offered.

"Yeah, I think that's probably going to put an emphatic end to my political aspirations."

"I'd vote for ya."

"No offense, but it doesn't sound like your political career had much traction anyway," Rogers added.

Silent the *entire* time was Henry Whitman. Until now.

"Matt. You could have done anything you wanted," Henry said.

"Whoaaa. Fred MacMurray. You're alive. You his dad?" Mo asked.

"No. I was his Headmaster in high school," Henry answered solemnly.

"No shit. Since you used the term "Headmaster" instead of "Principal", I'm assuming that was at some prep school like Deerfield or Andover. Some shit like that."

"Choate."

"You still at Choate, Dr. MacMurray?"

"He's the President of Yale now," Matt interjected.

"No *shit.* I've been to Yale. Gave a speech to the senior class like 5-6 years ago," Mo said.

"Seven," Henry responded.

"You remember it?"

"It was kind of difficult to forget. 72 F Bombs in 30 minutes. One of the faculty members counted."

"You request the bull, you get the horns," Mo said, making the matching symbol with his thumb and pinky.

"The students requested you. If I'm not mistaken, your last words were, "Fuck authority. Fuck a lot of people. Smoke a lot of pot. And try crack at least once in your life."

Mo saw no need to apologize. "That's sound advice. How'd you end up here? Smack someone across the head with a hardcover copy of The Great Gatsby?"

Henry looked up for the first time. "I made the worst decision of my life."

"Guys like you don't make bad decisions," Mo said. "I'll show you some bad decisions."

Henry hesitated to share with these mostly complete strangers. He couldn't bear the thought of even saying it out loud. "I destroyed evidence of one of my employees getting sexually harassed by her superior."

Matt looked more disappointed than a six year old finding out there wasn't really a Santa Claus. "Why'd you do it?" he asked.

"I don't know," was Henry's response. "Actually, that's not true. I do know. The way I saw it, I had four choices. Ignore it, and hope the girl eventually quit. With no evidence to support her claims, she would have had a difficult time proving anything. But heaven forbid if she could," he continued with his voice trailing off. "I could offer to buy her silence by paying her off with a confidentiality clause that would prevent her from talking about it to anyone. She needed money, so that was an appealing option, although getting approval from the Board of Directors without a proper explanation, would have been difficult. I could have fired the guy on the spot. But that would likely have resulted in a very ugly, very public mess that the media would pounce on. The statement that 'there's no such thing as bad publicity' definitely does not apply to institutions of higher learning. And lastly, I could have tried to force the guy into an early retirement. That wouldn't have been easy though. Don is only 51, and he would not have gone down without a fight—even with a nice severance package, and a reference for future employment while staring at a memory card full of evidence. And if he fought it, things could have gotten really ugly. My whole life, I lived by the code my father taught me. Be honest at all times. Treat people the way you would want to be treated. And help those that cannot help themselves. And yet, when faced with the most important decision of my life, I couldn't make myself do it. I'm a disgrace."

"Then fix it," Matt said simply.

"It's too late for that. The horse is already out of the barn. The good thing is that Don will get fired, but it won't be because of anything I did. The school is going to get a horrible black eye. I'll lose my job, and probably my pension. But that's ok. I deserve it. But my wife doesn't deserve this. And I don't know how I'm ever going to look her and my daughter in the face when they ask me why I didn't help this girl."

None of them had a response for Henry. No one knew what to say. Until Mo decided to ever so delicately break the silence.

"Yeah, you're fucked," he said.

Rogers glared at him as if to say, "Really?"

"What? It's true. He's fucked."

"You've never made a decision you regret, Mo?"

"Nope."

"How is that even possible?" Matt asked.

"Because I live by the Principle of the Moment."

"What kind of bullshit philosophy is that?" Rogers demanded to know.

"It's based on an ancient Chinese Proverb that looks at life as a series of moments. And since we don't know if we'll even be alive tomorrow, why should we worry about it? Worry about the day at hand. So every decision I make is based solely on what is best for me at that very moment. If I think my boss is an asshole, I tell him. If I want to go to South Beach, I go. If I feel like signing autographs, I sign. If I want to sleep with a woman, or smoke a vial of crack, I do."

"No matter who it hurts?" Matt asked.

"Who am I hurting?"

"Well, the women for starters."

"I don't lie to them," Mo explained. "If they ask if I plan to call them after sleeping with 'em, I tell them 'probably not, unless I'm wasted.'"

"And if they don't ask?"

Mo smiled. "I'm like the Army. Don't ask, don't tell."

"That sounds like a real great philosophy,"

Rogers said, shaking his head.

"It's served me well so far. I'm rich. I'm famous. And I'm rich."

"Money isn't everything."

"Says the man who makes 21 mill a year."

"So I should know what I'm talking about."

"Not unless you've never had money. And my guess is you've always had it. Probably never worked a day in your life. No job while in school. No summer job cutting lawns. Hell, you don't even have a job now."

"How do you figure?"

"Just because they pay you, doesn't make it a job. They don't say you "work" baseball. You "play" it."

"It's the law of supply and demand," Rogers said, defending himself. "If people wanted to pay money to watch Hector wash cars, then he'd make 21 mill a year."

"That's messed up," Mo said.

"He's right," Hector answered.

"It's still messed up."

"As if what you do is a real job?" Rogers asked.

"I'm a pretender. My job is to pretend to be someone I'm not. But the difference between you and me is I understand that I'm ridiculously overpaid."

"You don't know anything about me. My father was a salesman. My mother is a teacher. When I wasn't studying or playing baseball, I was working two different jobs because my father insisted I was going to a good college regardless of how things turned out with baseball. But my senior year, my dad died and my sister and I were forced to live on my mom's $40,000 a year salary. We were about to lose our house, and even though I had scholarship offers, there was no money for my sister to go to college. So when I got drafted by the Cubs and offered a $200,000 signing bonus, I took it. We used the money to pay off the house and send my sister to school, and I toiled around the minors for nearly seven years before making it to the majors. So yeah, I have money now, but I didn't always. And by making the choices I did, I did the two things my father would have hated most."

"Not going to college...*and*--?" Matt asked.

"Playing for the Cubs."

A light bulb went off in Matt's head. He nodded. "Rogers. As in Rogers Hornsby. Your old man was a Cardinals' fan."

"The Cubs most hated rival," Rogers said.

"I'm sure he would have understood," Matt offered.

"You don't know my father."

"That's true. But he sounds a bit like mine. Ironically, my dad wanted me to be a baseball player, but I couldn't hit a curve ball. First time I ever faced one was in high school. I batted leadoff and could have sworn the pitch was coming straight for my head. I threw my bat in the air and dove backwards; only to find that the pitch had broken across the plate for a strike. As I dusted myself off, I heard everyone laughing—fans, teammates, the other team— and I knew my baseball career would be short-lived.

But I was actually a pretty good basketball player. Not that my dad ever let me enjoy it. He was constantly on me to work on my game. In the morning before school, and then again after practice at night. He made me hate the game so much that I stopped practicing altogether, which incensed him. One day we were playing our biggest rival, and I hit a seventy-five foot shot to win the game at the buzzer, and everyone stormed the court in celebration. As I was sprinting toward the locker room with my fist in the air I heard him shout out, "Yeah, but you can't make a free throw! I never played another game."

"Just to spite your old man?" Rogers asked.

"Yup. I did everything to spite him. He wasn't even a bad guy. But he had my life planned out for me. Which schools I would attend. What sports I would play. What job I would have. And man, did he hate my job. Thought financial guys sold "perception" over reality and that we were all crooks. I didn't even disagree with him, but I never let him know that. Wasn't about to give him the satisfaction. And then, the day after he died, I quit my job. Decided I wanted to do something important with my life."

"And you went into politics?!" Mo laughed. "Man, there are more crooks in D.C. than in Attica."

"I wanted to be different. Started out on the Board of Ed in our town. Then ran for Mayor. Then decided to run for Governor. Thought all you needed was some good ideas and enough money to get those ideas out, but I was wrong on both counts. They shouldn't have a Political Science major in college. It should be Political Math. Because that's what an election is. It's a math equation. 2% of the population pay over 30% of the taxes. 47% of the population don't pay any taxes at all. 52% of the population is pro life, but only 88% of those people pay taxes. 93% of the people make less than $100,000 a year; 46% of those people are pro life. So if you only raise taxes on those making more than $100K a year and take a pro life stance, you've got 43% of the vote. Raising the minimum wage gets you some younger votes, but loses the small business owners who have to pay it. So what you need to figure out is how many of those small business owner votes you already have. To be safe, you raise the minimum wage *and* cut out luxury taxes and pick up another 10% of the vote. Then you take a hard line stance on illegal immigrants—no offense, Hector—"

Hector nodded. None taken.

"--and pick up a few more votes. But the most important thing when pandering is to only pander to those who actually get out and vote. Of course, none of these things help reduce the deficit, but as long as you get elected, who cares?"

"Then how come you didn't?"

"Because Matt has too much integrity to play that game," Henry said.

"Says the man who allowed one of his employees to get sexually harassed and demeaned by her boss."

"Mo, that's out of line," Matt responded.

"He's right. I made every right decision in my life, except for the one that mattered most."

"That's great that you're beating yourself up and all, but when you get out of here, how bout you do something about it?" Rogers said.

"What can I do?" Henry asked. "They already know everything."

"Apologize to the girl for starters. Volunteer at a homeless shelter. Run a fundraiser for abused women."

"This coming from the man who blows by children looking for autographs like he's on the last lap of the Indy 500."

"Oh, and you sign everything thrust at you?"

"Every single one for children and hot women. Guys over 25?...No. They creep me out."

"I would think that signing autographs would be cool," Matt said.

"It is. For the first thousand of them. But after you sign 200 a day, it gets old really quickly."

"Sign your name 200 times a day and collect 21 million dollars a year?" Hector interjected. "Where do I sign up?"

"I'm sure it all sounds great, but picture yourself out to dinner with your wife or your girlfriend, and you're having an argument when someone comes up and sticks a piece of paper and a pen in your face. *You* have a bad day and maybe two people think you're an asshole. But I have a bad day and it ends up in the newspaper in the morning, and two *million* people think I'm an asshole."

"I guess everyone's problems are relative," Matt lamented.

"What about you, Chico? There's got to be

more to your story. A former lawyer who's washing cars now? What gives?" Mo asked.

Hector mulled it over. Carefully considered how much he really wanted to share. "I was a lawyer in Juarez, Mexico," he said at last. "A defense attorney who made my living defending wealthy foreigners who managed to get themselves into trouble so I could afford to take on poor clients who really needed my help."

"Where the hell were you when I needed you?" Mo groaned.

"You should have called me. It was a pretty good living. Had a wife and daughter and a nice house. But Juarez eventually became like a war zone where the cartels fought for territory since it borders on El Paso, Texas. It became a dangerous place to live. The Federales were powerless to do much, and anyone with money became a target." He paused a moment to compose himself before continuing, "One night while we were sleeping, two men broke into our house. I heard my wife and daughter's screams while I was getting a drink of water and grabbed the shotgun that I kept in my office. I killed them both on two shots. Blew a hole in the second one's chest from about five feet away, so wide you could see through it. They were messengers from one of the cartels to get me to drop a case I was working on. I knew we weren't safe, so I packed a bag, we crossed the border under the cover of night, and kept heading north. I had no way to get to my money, and I could never return. My law degree isn't worth the paper it was printed on up here, so I took any job I could get. And now that I've been arrested, I'll be deported, and I'll be dead within 24 hours after being sent back to Mexico."

Stunned silence. Not one of them had expected that story.

As usual, Mo broke the silence. "Damn, brah. If I were you, I'd be asking everyone for their shoelaces so I could make a noose."

"Don't think the thought hasn't crossed my mind. But I couldn't do that to my wife and daughter. They'd only blame themselves."

No one wanted to look in his direction. Rogers looked away. O'Malley took a deep breath and released it slowly. Henry fiddled with his thumbs. He didn't feel quite as badly suddenly. The silence was finally broken by the sound of heavy shoes pounding down the hallway.

A guard stood in front of the door as it slid open.

"Let's go," he said.

"Which one of us?" Mo asked.

"All of you," was the answer.

VII.
the knights of redemption

"We all made bail?" Matt asked as they were being ushered down the corridor.

"Not exactly," the guard responded.

A steel door opened at the end of the hallway, opening to a concrete tunnel. A golf cart towing a tram awaited them.

"Where are we going?" Rogers demanded.

"You'll find out soon enough," the guard answered.

"What if we make a break for it?" Mo smirked.

The metal door slammed shut behind them. There didn't appear to be any other way out.

"Where are you going to go?"

"What kind of messed up jail is this?" Mo said. "I want my phone call."

"You're about to get it."

"Let's go," the driver urged impatiently.

No one seemed very comfortable with the situation, but they were intrigued.

"You realize if I go missing, people are going to look for me," Mo announced.

"If you go missing, they'll make it a holiday," Rogers cracked.

"Look who's talking, Mr. 50 Home Run Guy That Nobody Wants. How big of a dick do you have to be to hit 52 home runs in a season and still nobody wants you?" Mo answered.

Two turns and about a half mile of tunnel later, the tram eased to a stop in front of another door. A man waited outside. Shirt and tie. Dress slacks. Could have been a detective or maybe FBI.

Inside, there were five rooms, with a nearly identically dressed man standing in front of each. The person leading them in pointed to Door #1.

"Mr. O'Malley. Room 1," the man said. He continued to point to each door as he spoke. "Mr. Falls. Room 2. Mr. Conners. Room 3. Mr. Rodriguez. Room 4. Mr. Whitman. Room 5."

Matt waited for each of the others to disappear into their rooms before he entered his. It looked like a typical interrogation room. Concrete floors. Cinderblock walls. A metal table sat in the center of the room with metal chairs on two sides of it.

The man pointed to one of the chairs and motioned for Matt to sit.

* * *

"What's this about?" Matt questioned.

"Consider this....your phone call," the man responded cryptically.

* * *

"You cops?" Mo asked.

"Not cops."

* * *

"We're scientists," one of the men told Rogers.

* * *

Hector eyed his man suspiciously. "For the government?"

"We're privately funded."

* * *

Henry still looked defeated.

"We work for you actually,"

"At Yale?" Henry asked, puzzled.

"Yes. And we'd prefer to keep it that way," the man replied.

* * *

"What does this have to do with us?" Matt pressed.

"Have you ever had a decision you wished you could do over?"

"I don't know. Maybe."

* * *

"No," Mo insisted.

* * *

"Sure," Rogers answered.

* * *

"Hasn't everyone?" Hector asked.

* * *

"Everyone has," Henry affirmed.

* * *

"Well, we're the people that can help you do that," the man told Matt.

* * *

"You have a Delorean?" Mo asked sarcastically.

"Not a Delorean," the man laughed.

"A time machine transports your body. We transport your mind."

* * *

"The human mind has millions of memories stored inside it; most of which we don't even know we have," he explained to Hector. "We have the ability to tap into any one of those memories at the exact moment it was established, so you can alter your decision."

* * *

"Of course when you change it, everything that occurred after it, changes with it."

Henry stared at him, wanting desperately to believe him, but failing to see how it could be.

* * *

"But why us?" Matt persisted.

"You each sounded like you had a regret or two."

* * *

"You were listening in on us?"

"Honestly?" the man in Mo's room asked.

"No. Lie to me."

"Yes, we were."

"Isn't that illegal?"

"It might be. If we actually existed."

* * *

"No one knows we exist, Henry. We like to call ourselves The Knights of Redemption."

* * *

"Knights of what?" Mo asked.

"Redemption."

* * *

Matt leaned back in his chair--intrigued. Absorbing it all. "Let's say I believed you," he said. "Which I don't. But let's pretend I did. How exactly would this work?"

"You'd put on that headset, relax, and think back to a moment you wish you could change. And that device will take you there."

"Just like that?"

"Just like that." The man sensed skepticism. "Don't believe me? Let me show you."

He took the headset from Matt and put it on. It looked like a cross between a pair of Beats and a leather old-school, football helmet. A wire jutted out of one of the ear pieces and plugged snugly into a small metal box with an assortment of dials, screens, buttons and lights on it. It looked slightly less complicated than Matt thought perhaps it should have been, in order to accomplish what they claimed.

"You see this pencil?" The scientist held it up in front of him.

"Yes. And?"

The man snapped it in two.

"Oooohhh. Impressive. You broke a pencil." Matt wasn't impressed.

The man held up the unbroken pencil in front of him.

"Did I?"

"Is that a magic pencil?"

"See for yourself." He handed it over, and Matt examined it with the scrutiny of an IRS agent. He couldn't find a thing wrong with it.

* * *

On of the Knights stood in front of Henry. "What am I wearing?" he asked.

"Clothes."

"Specifically," the man insisted.

Henry decided to play along. "White shirt. Khakis. Blue tie."

"You sure about that?"

The man was suddenly wearing a pink shirt, navy pants and no tie. Henry's eyes seemed to be playing tricks on him. He rubbed them for clarity, but it didn't help.

* * *

Hector stared at the man before him.

"Where am I sitting?" the man goaded.

"In front of me."

"Am I really?"

The man was now standing behind Hector, who spun around to find him. It was like tracking a Mig fighter.

"Whoa!" was all Hector could manage to utter.

* * *

"What about this table?"

"What about it?" Mo asked.

The table was instantly flipped on its flat side. Mo didn't see it getting flipped. It just suddenly was.

He jumped up. Pointed to the table accusingly. "It wasn't upside down when we walked in, was it?!"

"No, it wasn't," Knight #2 smiled.

"That is some freaky shit."

* * *

"Do me a favor. Place both of your arms on the table in front of you," Knight #3 asked Rogers.

Rogers grudgingly did so.

In the blink of an eye, his right arm was now handcuffed to the bottom of his chair, with Rogers yanking frantically to free it to no avail.

"What the hell?! You a magician??"

"Magicians are illusionists," the Knight responded. "We deal with science."

* * *

The man held up the headset. "Try it out," he said to Matt. "Start with something small and insignificant. Nothing that will change the course of your life. That's for later."

"Ok. I'll play along," Matt relented. "This morning I forgot my wallet. Which is why I didn't have any identification on me when I was brought in."

"Perfect. Put on the headset and think back to when you left your house this morning. Only this time—grab it in your mind."

Matt chuckled. "Sure thing." He started to put it on, only to stop. "This isn't going to electrocute me is it? Like old school electric shock treatment."

"It will be nothing like that. You won't feel a thing. It's like an MRI of your mind."

Matt put it on and dropped deep in thought for about five seconds. He opened his eyes and took off the headset.

"All set?"

"Yup."

The man spoke into the intercom on the desk. "Jimmy, get me Mr. O'Malley's personals."

The person on the other end of the intercom entered a moment later carrying a manila envelope. The Knight reached inside and pulled out a set of keys. Then a wallet. He held it up with a smile.

* * *

"I'm wearing one grey sock and one black one right now," Rogers said as he put on the headset. "People were making fun of me for it all day."

The man motioned with his head for Rogers to look down. He lifted his pant legs. Both socks were now black.

* * *

"I left my watch on the nightstand in my hotel room this morning," Mo said, fitting the headset snugly over his baseball cap. He closed his eyes.

By the time he opened them again, an assistant was removing a gold watch from an envelope.

* * *

"I take off my wedding band every morning when I shower, so I won't get soap in it. Half the time I forget to put it back on and my wife gets upset with me."

"Close your eyes."

Henry did as instructed.

"Is this what you were missing?" the man asked as he held up a platinum wedding band.

* * *

"I cut myself shaving. This nick..." Hector said as he pointed to his chin, "took 40 minutes to stop *bleeding."*

A minute or so later, Hector ran his hand over his face. Smooth as a baby's bottom. Not a single nick.

* * *

Matt seemed to be having some second thoughts.

"Still don't believe me?"

"This is crazy. But if you guys can do this, why not use it to prevent great tragedies like 9/11 or WWII?"

"We actually tried to at first," the man explained, "but we found two things: 1) Every decision comes with its own unique set of consequences and 2) You can only change your own mind. You can prevent someone from doing something, but where there's evil, it will only manifest itself in other ways. When we prevented 9/11, Al Queda ended up crashing a subway car into Grand Central Terminal and killed five times as many people."

* * *

"Riddle me this, Batman. I remember that the table was right side up when we walked in. I remember that I left my watch in the hotel."

"Do you?"

"Pretty sure."

"You know about us, and you're having doubts. Imagine someone who doesn't know we exist."

"They'll just think they're going crazy," Mo said.

"Only until they wake up the next day. And

then that memory will be archived away in the vault that is their mind. By the next morning, they'll only remember their new life."

* * *

"So if I went back and decided to go to the prom with the girl I blew off to go drinking in the parking lot with my buddies, she wouldn't remember what I did?" Matt asked.

"She might be a bit confused at first, but think it was a bad dream. Once she woke up the next day, it would be as if it never happened."

* * *

"Let's say I did this. Do I re-live the past 20 years?"

"Your body stays in the present, Rogers. You zip in mentally. Make a change. And wake up."

"Wake up right here? In this very chair?"

"Well...not necessarily."

"Not necessarily?!"

"I mean, you could. But every changed decision will usually result in a number of changed circumstances that follow. Your life might be completely different."

"I'm not following you."

"You would wake up wherever your life took you at the exact same moment we are in right now."

"Then I guess I'll see you when I see you," Rogers said as he slipped the headset back on.

"Good luck," the man responded.

"That sounds a bit ominous."

The man smiled. "Everything will be fine. And if it isn't, you can always fix it."

"How can I find you?" Rogers asked.
"Don't worry. We'll find you."

* * *

Matt paced across the room in thought. Decided he didn't have much to lose. If it was a dream, it was a cool one that he'd be a little sad to wake up from. But if it was real, the possibilities were endless.

"Let's do this," he said at last.

VIII.
delaney

The very qualities that would one day make Delaney Elliott desirable, caused her to be mostly alone in high school. She was beautiful, smart, funny, sweet, and came from one of the wealthiest families at Choate, but high school boys were only interested in the first one. In fact, if they were honest, boys would admit to wanting a girl they could bring home to mother, but when mom wasn't around, the girl needed to be sexy and forward. Not so much so as to be considered dirty, but enough to offset the fact that most teenage boys were shy and awkward.

So girls found themselves walking the tightrope between being girl next doorish and closet whores, not even realizing that even those who successfully managed to do it, wouldn't be successful for long. High school boys, above all else, had the attention span of a coonhound in the woods—scampering off in a different direction anytime they stumbled onto a new scent.

So Delaney forged on alone, friends with guys, and secretly hated by jealous girls. But she moved forward with a belief—one that was reinforced by her parents--that one day, she would be the girl every man decided they wanted to be with the moment they laid eyes on her.

Her best friend throughout high school had been Matt O'Malley. She thought he was cute, and he was certainly bright and athletic, but more than anything, he made her laugh. While guys were checking out female body parts, girls were looking for someone who made them laugh. It was a secret that would have saved Matt a great deal of heartache, had he learned it a few years earlier.

Instead, he stumbled forward as seemingly all boys did at his age, succeeding with girls when success came easily to him, never putting too much effort forward, and completely missing the obvious signs from his best friend.

A couple of months after high school, Delaney began dating an upperclassman from her college, whom she would later marry. Matt bounced through a couple of relationships before finally settling for a woman who was all wrong for him. The things that never bothered him when they were just friends--she was impatient, had virtually no sense of humor whatsoever, and hated animals—drove him insane when they began dating. Why he eventually asked her to marry him was a simple, if inglorious answer. He was the last remaining single person among his group of ten or so close friends, and he had visions of holidays and birthdays spent alone, or worse yet, as the third wheel among his married friends. On paper, Tara looked the part. She was attractive, smart and driven. That last quality could also have been viewed as a negative. A perfect example being that she supported his foray into politics, not because she believed in him as a person, but because if he had been successful, it would have lead a better life for them both. Their marriage was essentially loveless, with the exception of the once or twice a year lovemaking sessions where Tara would talk dirty to him, which usually resulted in him laughing out loud and the session ending before it began. It was a marriage headed straight for divorce, accelerated a bit when fate decided to intervene. Tara had crashed her car while sexting Matt's campaign manager from his failed Gubernatorial effort and the rest, as they say, was history.

If you were to ask him, Matt could tell you the day his life took a turn for the drastically awful, and he had no one to blame but himself. It was spring of his senior year of high school, and Delaney asked him to the prom. He turned her down, not because he didn't think she was cute. Not because he didn't like her as a person. Not because he liked someone else more. But because he had already made plans to get drunk with his buddies and then go to the prom with them. Matt thought he was doing the right thing by honoring his commitment, not realizing that any one of his guy friends would have cancelled on him for a six-pack of Pabst. That was just how most guys were wired, even if Matt wasn't, and the decision cost him endless ridicule for years afterward, for turning down the beautiful Grey Poupon mustard heiress. He didn't disagree with the criticism, but of course that realization also didn't come until much later as well.

The headset in place, Matt scoured his memory banks for the moment Delaney had asked him to the prom, but wasn't sure exactly when and where that was. He knew it had been just a few days before it, but couldn't for the life of him remember where the conversation had taken place. He supposed it was his mind's way of self-preservation— trying to forever forget the idiotic decisions he had made when he was younger.

And then finally, it came to him. He had just walked off the baseball field following a game where he had been a reluctant hero and found Delaney sitting on the hood of his car.

"Nice game," she said.

"What game were you watching? I struck out three times."

"But you drove in the winning run."

Matt laughed, "Only because I got hit in the foot by a pitch while trying to bail out of the batter's box."

"Sometimes it's about being in the right place at the right time," she smiled.

"I don't know why you even waste your time watching me play. I'm horrible."

"Because we're friends."

"So you agree that I'm horrible."

"That's not what I said."

"But that's what you *meant*."

"What I meant was that it wouldn't matter to

me if you were horrible, *because* we're friends. Besides, I think you have a lot of potential, Mr. O'Malley."

"That sounds like a backhanded compliment if I've ever heard one," he laughed.

"Stop trying to make everything I say sound like a bad thing!"

"So you think I have potential as a baseball player?"

"Let me put it this way. I don't think we'll be seeing you play at Citi Field anytime soon. But I do think you have tremendous potential as a person."

"And on what are you basing this assessment of me?"

"Because you like to help people. That alone puts you ahead of 98% of the population. Most people are only interested in helping themselves," she explained.

He wasn't really buying it. "I guess."

"So we're out of here in a few weeks. What career path are you going to pursue to that will maximize your ability to help people? I know you've already got it all planned out."

"What makes you so sure of that?"

"Because you plan *everything*."

"I was thinking maybe I'd go into politics. I could be the world's first honest politician."

"You're too nice for politics," she reasoned.

"I'm not *that nice*."

"Yes, you are. But I mean that as a compliment."

"Well, thank you," Matt said, as he opened the

door to his car. "You need a lift?"

"Obviously," Delaney laughed. "You think I was waiting around here for my health? I hate baseball."

"Then get in. Before I change my mind, smart ass."

"On a somewhat serious note," she began, "I have a question to ask you."

She was fidgeting with the air vents while she spoke. It was unusual for her to be nervous about much.

"And what's that?"

She blushed a bit. Fumbled with her house keys. "So seeing how neither of us have a date for the prom thingy this weekend...I was wondering if maybe you'd like to go with me?"

"You mean like, together?"

"Well, yeah, although I suppose we could take separate cars if you'd rather..." she answered sarcastically.

"No, it's not that. I just don't understand how someone like you doesn't already have a date."

And what exactly do you mean by *someone like me?*"

"I mean, you're pretty, smart—"

"Do you mean I'm *pretty smart* or pretty *and* smart?"

"And," Matt laughed.

She brightened. "You think I'm pretty?"

"I don't really think that's up for debate. I think it's more or less accepted as fact."

"In that case, thank you. And in answer to

your question, I guess it's because I'm a fast runner."

"Excuse me?"

"Anytime I saw a guy that I thought might ask me to prom, I ran away."

"Well, aren't you popular?" he remarked. "Running away from all these guys that wanted to ask you to prom. Must be nice to be so popular!"

"You said yourself, it's considered a fact that I'm pretty," she shot back, sticking her tongue out at him.

"I thought I saw you duck down a hallway when you saw me earlier."

"I wouldn't have run from you. You were the reason I ran from everyone else."

"And why's that?"

"Because I was hoping you were going to ask me, dumbass."

"Really? I had no idea."

"That's because you're a guy. It's widely accepted that guys are stupid."

"Apparently so," he chuckled.

"Well....?"

"Well what?"

"Oh my god, I'm going to kill you," she said.

He pulled up in front of her house and shifted into *Park*.

"Here's the thing. I promised the boys we'd all go solo and get hammered before the dance."

"Oh." She had a hard time concealing her disappointment. "So that would be a '*no*' then."

Matt smiled broadly and winked at her. "That

would be an '*absolutely*'. I can get drunk with them anytime."

IX.
mr. baseball

With the exception of convincing Bea Whitton to marry him, Rogers Conner's father wanted his son to go to college and play for the Cardinals more than any two things in his life. Unfortunately, a heart attack—more specifically five donuts a day along with plentiful helpings of bacon—robbed him of his opportunity to see how his son turned out as an adult. Rogers was fairly certain he wouldn't have been pleased.

The last game his father ever saw him play, Rogers hit two home runs and fouled off a pitch that practically landed in Mr. Conner's lap. His father held up the ball and Rogers nodded at him in the reserved, non-descript way boys communicated with their fathers, before homering on the next pitch. After the game, when a scout from the Cubs told them they had their eye on drafting him in next year's draft, Mr. Conner politely, but firmly responded by saying, "Rogers is going to college, Mr. Mannetti, so don't waste your pick on him."

Once the man had shaken hands and left, Rogers asked, "Did you only tell him that because you hate the Cubs?"

"I told him that," his father responded, "because you're going to college. You have to promise me two things. The first, is that if something happens to me, you will go to college and graduate."

"Nothing's going to happen to you, dad. You're strong like bull."

"Just promise me," he urged ominously.

"Ok, dad. I promise."

"The second thing is promise me you'll never play for the Cubs."

"You got it," Rogers laughed.

It was only time he had ever lied to his father.

The problem was that after his father died, money was tight, and the only way Rogers' sister would have been able to go to college, was if he paid for it. So he signed with the Cubs and broke both promises to his father with one swipe of a pen.

As he sat in the metal chair in a room far below the jailhouse up above, wearing a leather headset with suction cups that fired electric volts into his brain, he rewound the images in his mind like a person using a DVR, until he settled on the very morning he had signed with the Cubs. His mother was sipping a cup of jet black coffee before work.

"So have you decided what you're going to do?" she asked, looking up from the morning newspaper she was reading. "Are you going to sign with the Cubs?"

"Dad would have hated that," he replied.

"He would have hated it, but he would have

understood."

"He always wanted Sam and I to go to college."

"Well, that's certainly an option," Mrs. Conner said. "For you at least."

"What about Sam?" Rogers asked.

"She'll qualify for some academic money as well as need based, but money's tight. She'll probably have to go to a junior college or state school if she wants to go."

"She's too good for that, mom."

"We just don't have many choices is the problem. Besides, it's not where you go; it's what you do when you're there."

Rogers paced across the kitchen. "Let me ask you something. Would we be able to survive for the next four years or so financially if both Sam and I went to college? Pay the mortgage, the bills, food, gas..."

"We could," she answered, "But it would be tight."

"So you think I should sign with the Cubs."

It wasn't clear from her voice and demeanor what she thought he should do. Her words indicated one thing, but her tone said something completely different altogether. "I think you should do whatever you want to do. You've earned that right. And we'll work it out either way."

Rogers washed his cereal bowl out in the sink and stuck it in the dishwasher.

"I've actually got an idea," he said at last.

"Care to share it with me?"

"I will if it works."

He kissed her on the cheek and left.

Twenty minutes later, he pulled onto the campus of Choate Rosemary Hall. The prep school campus more closely resembled a college than a high school. Sprawling lawns. Majestic brick buildings. Rogers pulled his 1985 Pontiac Firebird into a parking spot between a Mercedes and Porsche in front of the athletic center and was greeted by two people.

"Rogers. I'm Anthony Fallacaro," the older man said. He was tall and muscular with a thick head of hair that was at one time black, but now had a fair amount of grey sprinkled in. He was distinguished and yet rough looking at the same time the result of a tough upbringing in the Bronx crossed with years as the baseball coach at one of the most elite prep schools in the country. "And this is Matt O'Malley, our Senior Captain."

"Don't let the title fool you. I'm a pretty horrific baseball player," Matt said.

"But an excellent leader of men," Anthony laughed.

Rogers shook both of their hands. "Nice to meet you. I appreciate you taking the time to meet with me."

"Have to be honest. I was a little surprised to get your call. I know the Cubs drafted you."

"Well, I'm trying not to be as my dad used to say, 'Penny wise and pound foolish'," Rogers said.

"Your dad was a good man. We went way back. Coached little league against each other for years."

"He was a good man," Rogers agreed. "And he always wanted me to go to college."

"Most people do a PG year to help them get into college, but from what I hear, you've already got plenty of options on that front as well."

"I do and I don't. There's a little hitch in my giddyup so to speak."

"It just so happens that the person who oversees our hitch in the giddyup department happens to be our Head of School and we have a meeting with him in five minutes," Anthony laughed.

"Perfect."

The office of the Head of School was everything you would expect from a person in his position. Cherry wood furniture and crown molding. Expensive oriental rugs. Ornate decorative curtains partially covering windows that looked out onto the quad.

"Dr. Whitman," Anthony began, "I'd like you to meet Rogers Conner. He's widely considered to be the best baseball player in the state of Connecticut. And you know Matt O'Malley of course."

"Welcome," Henry exclaimed motioning for everyone to sit. He was carefree and relaxed at this point in his life. A young looking forty-eight years old. "Everyone grab a seat and relax. So how can I help?"

"Well, Rogers is interested in doing a Post Grad year here at Choate, but finances are an issue," Anthony explained.

"I can certainly look into it, but I'm afraid I can't promise anything."

"There is...one other catch," Rogers said slowly.

"There always is," Henry smiled.

"I need my sister to be admitted as well. She'll be a junior this fall and she has always had her heart set on Yale. It's the best school and it has one of the largest need-based endowments. She's brilliant, but as we all know, brilliant isn't always enough to get into Yale. I think Choate could be the edge she needs to get in."

Anthony looked on anxiously.

"That could pose a bit more of a problem," Henry said. He didn't say it in a nasty way. It was more matter-of-fact than anything.

"I assure you that she would be the better end of this deal. There is no question in my mind that one day, she would end up being one of the most distinguished alums to ever graduate from Choate."

"It's not that I don't believe you. It's just the timing is tough. Most of our scholarship money has already been given out for the year. I'd need to go to the board of directors to see if I could get special permission to tap further into the endowment."

"And what are the chances of that?" Anthony asked.

"I'd say it could go either way, Fal."

"If you decide to try, feel free to let them know that I will smash three home runs against Deerfield so far, that they will need to dig up Lewis and Clark just to find the balls," Rogers promised.

He had hit the magic button. Broad smiles from all in the room. Anything to beat their oldest rival.

"I'll be in touch," Henry said as he rose to shake the hand of the man that would one day be known in Choate circles as *Mr. Baseball.*

X.
the mexican lawyer

Mo's arms were crossed in front of his chest. His scientist looked flummoxed. They looked like they had been at this for a while.

"Look, if you want me to try your invention thing, I'll try it. I'm always up for trying new things. I just don't know what I'd use it for."

"How can you not have any regrets?" the man asked, exasperated.

"I just don't. Everything's a learning experience. If I didn't make bad decisions, how would I know what good ones were?"

There was a sorted of twisted logic to what he said.

"Don't regret walking off the #1 TV show in the country?"

"Nope."

"Don't regret getting arrested last night?"

"That was just a mistake. To be honest, I don't even remember putting them there in the first place."

"Don't regret getting arrested in Mexico?"

"Nah," Mo smiled, "It was a helluva party. "But..."

"But what?"

"But I should have gotten a better lawyer."

The man smiled and held out the headset. That was what he had been waiting to hear.

* * *

The trip south of the border had started as most of Mo's nights out had—without much thought. Two Bloody Mary's into his Saturday morning at a Malibu beach bar, someone brought up the idea of going to Vegas. Mo considered that a tired idea, having already ended up there five times in the last month. But six or seven drinks, four hours, and three bars later, someone suggested Tijuana, and that was all it took. Mo rented one of those party buses that you would normally find shuttling people from the airport terminal to the rental car lot by having the owner dragged out of a birthday party and throwing an extra five grand his way.

An hour later, they had a driver pick them up from the back alley behind the bar, and twenty-five people—including some complete strangers—were on their way to Mexico. What Mo failed to consider was that drug laws in Mexico were as stringent as drugs were plentiful. After doing several lines of blow in a not very clean bathroom, Mo found himself in the middle of a raid. He thought they were looking for underage drinkers as they did in the states, but they were actually looking for wealthy Americans that could afford to pay their way out of trouble. After finding a little bit of coke, and a lot of marijuana in his jacket pocket, Mo's party bus was headed back to the states without him.

For all that he had heard about Mexican prisons, what he found was quite a bit different. Yes, there were some awful, run-down, filthy, dangerous ones, but unlike in the states, where the seriousness of the crime determined the prison you were sent to, in Mexico, how fat your wallet was determined where you went.

Mo's prison cell resembled a studio apartment. Velvet couches. Sizeable bed. Nightstand. Reading lamp. In fact, the only visual clue it was actually a prison, was the guard that stood outside the door while Mo's attorney visited.

"This is your cell? It's nicer than most apartments I've lived in," Tommy Carter remarked.

"It's costing me a lot of money, Tommy, but everything's for sale down here. Everything except an innocent verdict that is. If you don't have money, they don't care about you. And if you do, they see it as a way to *make* money off you. They'll keep you as long as they can," Mo answered.

"I'm sorry I couldn't get you released prior to the trial, but they figured you'd just make a run for the border since you're so close."

"Two more weeks of this."

"Don't worry, I've made some progress. Might cost you some scratch, but I'll get you out of here. Need anything in the meantime?"

"I need you to find a guy named Hector Rodriguez. He's a lawyer down here who specializes in defending foreigners. When I need a contract negotiated, you're my guy. If I got caught with a hooker on Hollywood Boulevard, I know you could have it taken care of. No offense, Tommy, but this is a whole different world here, and from what I understand, this guy knows the system. Tell him we'll pay him whatever he wants. And don't take no for an answer."

"No problem. I'll take care of it," Tommy assured him. "How do I find him?"

"That's the thing. He lives in Juarez. You may need to go there."

"Jesus, Mo. That's a hella long way from here. Not to mention a veritable war zone. Granted you're sitting in jail, but I could get killed going there."

"Well, that's a chance I'm willing to take," Mo smiled.

"I'll try calling him first."

"Send the jet for him if need be. Just get him here. I'm getting hemorrhoids sitting on that hard toilet seat."

* * *

Meanwhile, at that very moment, in another life, Hector was struggling. He had the headset on, and a disturbed look on his face, with his eyes closed tightly. When his frustration got the better of him, he ripped the set off.

"I couldn't find it!" he exclaimed.

"What do you mean you couldn't find it?" his scientist asked.

"The memory I was searching for. It just kept taking me to some alternate life. A life I never experienced."

The knight looked puzzled. Bit down on the inside of his cheek in thought. "That has only happened once before."

"What does it mean?!" Hector asked in a panic.

"You can't find the memory because it no longer exists."

"How is that possible?? I didn't do anything. I didn't change anything."

"Someone else must have."

"But I thought you said we couldn't change anyone else's life? Only our own."

"I said you couldn't change it without their consent. This memory of yours—was it something you wanted to change anyway?"

"Obviously."

"Then whoever changed your life, must have done so with your consent. It must have been something you wanted to do."

"But—"

And then--WHOOOOSH. Just like that, Hector was gone from the room. Vanished into thin air. Like the table that was flipped upside down, one second he was there, and the next, he wasn't.

XI.
another life

Entertainers and Athletes Agency (EAA) was founded in the late 80's when four employees left the mailroom at the most successful talent and packaging agency in Hollywood and struck out on their own. What began as a boutique operation, exploded when Tom Cruise decided to go with them along with a previously little known actor named Kevin Costner, who burst onto the scene with a movie about Indians in the wild.

Within ten years, their client roster was a veritable Who's Who of Hollywood and their net income topped $400 million a year. Not satisfied with that, they then expanded to include representation for athletes, since so many of them crossed over into entertainment with endorsements and guest appearances on television and cameos in film. The irony of it all was that the very reason they started their own agency was because they felt their previous one had gotten so big, it lacked personal attention for the clients. They were now twice its size.

Nice, modern, and more artsy than lawyer-esque looking, Hector Rodriguez found himself seated in an oversized chair in his oversized office, with no idea whatsoever what he was doing there. The walls were decorated with framed pictures of him with famous people--the largest of which was one of him with none other than Mo Falls himself.

The room seemed to be spinning as he staggered back to his chair and Googled himself. A Wilkepedia article appeared instantly with 549,000 other results.

"Hector Rodriguez is a renowned talent agent at EAA (Entertainers and Athletes Agency) in Hollywood. A former attorney in Juarez, Mexico, he came to Hollywood at the request of one of his clients—5-time Tony Award, and Academy Award winning actor, Mo Falls. Rodriguez also represents a majority of Who's Who on Broadway, becoming an integral part as several transitioned to film. He lives in Brentwood with his wife, Lynn, and daughter, Hope."

Suddenly, there was a knock at the door. His assistant stuck her head in.

"Mo Falls is here to see you," she said.

Hector waved frantically. "Send him in! Send him in!"

Mo entered the room with a grin.

"What the hell is going on?!" Hector exclaimed.

"That's what I was hoping you were going to tell me, Chico!" Mo laughed.

"Wilkepedia says I'm a talent agent in

Hollywood."

"That would explain the office and the pictures," Mo said as he looked over the wall.

"It also says you're a five-time Tony Award winning actor. You played Phantom on Broadway for three years. You're the guy who succeeded Michael Crawford. Talk about a stretch."

"Actually not so much of one. My parents are both Broadway actors, and I went to the Eugene O'Neil School of Theatre to do exactly that. But...after I got into a bit of trouble, no productions would take me on. They said in the daily grind of Broadway, they needed someone more reliable."

"No kidding." Hector wouldn't have been more surprised if someone snuck up behind his chair and smashed him with a baseball bat.

"A family friend recommended me for a film, and from that I got the TV show. Anyway, I'm going to assume my bank account has taken a hit accordingly as well. Theatre is a passion, not a way to get rich."

Hector looked back at his computer screen.

"Not necessarily. This also says you won an Academy Award and that your last reported movie quote was $15 million."

"No shit?"

"What I don't get is how this happened? I went in to change the night the thugs broke into our house. Was going to clear out our bank accounts and move the family across the border. But when I went in to do that, I couldn't find the memory. Next thing I knew, I was here."

"Think I might be able to help you with that one, Chico. The guy kept badgering me, wondering how I didn't have any regrets. How there wasn't one thing in my life I would change. And on and on and on...So I thought about my time in the Mexican jail, and although it wasn't exactly hard time, it was kind of a waste. And then I remembered what you said about how you represented foreigners who got in trouble in Mexico, so I asked a friend to look you up."

"So I must have helped you get out of there, and in turn, you convinced me to bring my family to the states," Hector said, putting it all together.

"Talk about some crazy shit, huh? Those crazy ass scientists are playing with destiny. Who do they think they are?" Mo laughed.

"They can't make you do anything you didn't already want to do. We did this to ourselves."

The door to the elevator downstairs opened and Rogers Conner stepped into the lobby of EAA. Modern. Coldish. Marble floors and walls.

Sparsely decorated save for a couple of black leather sofas, a glass coffee table or two and a long marble receptionist desk behind which, four people sat manning the phones.

One of them jumped up upon seeing Rogers. "Mr. Conner! You don't need to check in at reception. You can just take the VIP elevator up to the 3rd floor. Jimmy is expecting you."

Even the VIP's apparently had VIP's.

"Where is his office again?" Rogers asked,

confused.

"Left off the elevator. Corner office on the right side." She seemed equally confused that he didn't remember.

"Thank you."

Rogers looked like a man more confused than any man had a right to be, until the elevator doors slid open and Mo Falls walked out, wearing his seemingly permanent grin. Their eyes locked for a brief instant and Rogers gave him a low, subtle wave, that Mo acknowledged with a smile and a nod. They didn't speak, but they communicated. There would be time to talk later.

Mo relished change. Lived for the daily curves life threw him. But Rogers liked stability. Even good surprises had always been jarring to him.

Rogers knocked on the door of the 3rd floor office as he entered. It was modern, but like Hector's office, had a wall of pictures that give it a warmer feeling. Almost half of them were of Rogers.

"Nice office, Jimbo."

"Isn't it? I have you to thank for that. I appreciate you putting pressure on them to bring me into EAA."

"I wasn't about to come here without you," Rogers said. He had a decidedly different personality now.

"You know it's funny, most people think that the offices with the best views are the ones that overlook the main lobby. But my office looks out at the VIP corridor. This week alone I've seen Lebron, Jeter, Peyton Manning, Joe Montana and the other day, I was zipping up my fly as I was coming out of the bathroom and walked right into Warren Beatty. You know what he said?"

Rogers was clearly getting a kick out of how excited his friend was. Small time agent turned big time.

"What?"

"He said, *'Careful big guy. You don't want to end up with the beans above the frank.'* Warren Fucking Beatty quoted "There's Something About Mary". How fucking cool is that?" Jimmy asked rhetorically.

"Pretty cool," Rogers smiled.

"So how was the Bel Air Hotel?"

"Nice I guess."

"You guess? You guess?!! Did you see Shaq? He was on his way in when I was on my way out."

"I don't think so. I must have missed him."

"You missed a 7 foot, 350 pound man? You need to get your eyes checked," Jimmy chuckled. "Anyway, this is what you're here to see. Chew on these numbers and see how they taste."

He handed him a cover sheet.

"What is it?"

"It's your retirement contract."

Rogers read it out loud. "Six years and 150 million dollars?"

"Yup."

"I'll be 40 by the time it's over. What if I don't last that long?"

"You don't have to," Jimmy explained. "You only have to play three more years. You can play longer if you want, but you need to only play three. After that, they'll make you a hitting instructor or manager either in the majors or their farm system just like you wanted."

"And they're going to pay me 25 million a year to do that?"

"Sort of. $100 million is paid over the first three years."

"Why would they do that?" Roger asked.

"Why? Because you're a fucking hero. You led us to the College World Series title at Notre Dame."

Rogers glanced at a picture of the two of them hugging and celebrating the NCAA championship while in college.

"You smashed a 405 foot home run off Jose Contreras in the 2000 Olympics to lead the US to the Gold Medal," Jimmy continued.

Rogers then saw a picture of himself with Derek Jeter and Tony Larussa in their USA jerseys at the World Baseball Classic.

"You led the Cardinals to two World Series titles."

Another picture with Larussa and Rogers. And one with Albert Pujols. And finally, a picture of Rogers and Jimmy as they held his 500th home run ball together.

"And you're going to retire among the top 10 all time in the majors in both home runs and RBIs. Once they ferret out those aholes on PEDs, you'll probably be top 5. But mostly, they're doing it out of loyalty. When all those other aholes left for bigger markets, you stayed. And they remembered."

It was almost a surreal feeling for Rogers to see pictures of himself from events he couldn't remember. He looked forward to the following morning when he could.

"So you ready to roll? he asked. We've got a plane waiting for us at LAX. We need to be in St. Louis by 4:00pm."

Jimmy grabbed his coat from behind the door and ushered Rogers into the hallway. Not expecting anyone to exit that particular door at that very moment, a young, female assistant stumbled in her heels and in the effort to catch her balance, sent a stack of papers flying to the floor. Some landed perfectly, like a jet landing on a runway. Others floated in the air, making their way to the ground like a hot air balloon coming in softly. She was rattled at this point. Bending over to pick up papers in heels and a skirt was as complicated as feeding a drawstring through a pair of sweatpants.

"I'm so sorry," Rogers said, bending down to help. "Please, let me get them for you."

He stacked them up neatly in a pile that was undoubtedly out of order, and offered them back to her.

"Thank you," she smiled, as she looked at the wedding band on his finger.

He hadn't noticed it himself until that moment.

"You, ok?" Jimmy asked.

"Uh...yeah...sure," was his disjointed reply.

XII.
thomas conner

Thomas Conner had spent his entire childhood and half his adult life in St Louis, until his boss informed him he was being transferred to Connecticut. He didn't want to go, but as a salesman without a college degree, he didn't have much choice. It turned out to be the best move of his life, as that was where he met his wife.

But while you could take the man out of St. Louis, you couldn't take St. Louis out of the man. He missed the down home folksiness of the Midwest. The somehow small town feel of a city with more than three million people. Most of all, he missed the sports teams, although when the football Cardinals left for Arizona in 1987, he became so disheartened that he stopped following the sport altogether and focused on the Cardinals baseball team.

Like his father, and his father's father before him, Thomas was a die-hard Cardinals fan. He knew their entire history, along with all the great players and managers who had worn the famed jersey with the two cardinals perched on a baseball bat. Stan Musial. Bob Gibson. Dizzy Dean. Lou Brock. Joe Torre. Whitey Herzog. Mark McGwire. Tony Larussa. And of course, his all-time favorite and the man his son was named after, Rogers Hornsby. The interesting thing was that "The Rajah" was widely considered to be a nasty player, not well-liked by opposing players and teammates alike. But Rogers had two qualities Thomas admired—consistency of effort and competitiveness—both of which he tried to drill into his son at an early age.

When the Cardinals won the World Series in 1967 and again in 1982, Thomas cried. When McGwire was accused of steroids in 1998, Thomas didn't speak to anyone for days. Unfortunately, he died before he had the chance to hear McGwire's apology years later, but Rogers was certain he would have forgiven him, because the most important quality to Thomas Conner, was forgiveness. It was that quality that Rogers was counting on should he run into his father in the afterlife, having failed to keep his promise to him. So when the opportunity arose to put right what he had once done wrong, Rogers jumped at the chance, not knowing exactly where his new path would lead him.

Where it led first was to Choate, where he made good on his promise to deliver three home runs against Deerfield en route to a thrashing they wouldn't soon forget. The following year, Rogers accepted a full scholarship to Notre Dame, a school that would have exceeded even his father's expectations. It was there that he met Jimmy Lawlor, the man who would one day become his agent. The two of them had been teammates on the only baseball team in Notre Dame history to win the College World Series. In the summer following his junior year, Rogers even managed to hit the game winning home run as the United States won the Gold medal in the 2000 Olympic games. Two years later, he was in the Cardinals farm system. The Cubs had traded away his rights after he decided to delay the pros for college.

He worked his way up through the minors one rung at a time, never spending more than four months at any one level. On his 24th birthday, exactly two years to the day before he had arrived in the majors in his previous life, he stepped onto the field at Busch Stadium for the first time. It was without question, a life altering experience, one he wished his father had been around to witness.

In 2006, his third season in the majors, he helped the Cardinals to their first World Series title in 24 years, after having beaten none other than the Cubs for the National League Pennant. Five years later, he would win another title, and was named both the National League and World Series MVP in the process. Quite simply, he was Midas—everything he touched, turned to gold.

That afternoon, Rogers hoisted his familiar #17 jersey over his head at what was likely to be the final major press conference for him before he retired.

"Rogers. How does it feel to know you'll most likely be ending your career in the same place it all started?" a reporter asked.

"My father's family is from St. Louis and there's something special about getting to play in front of your family and friends all the time. This city was my second home growing up, and it's the only home I've known as an adult. The only sad part about it is that my dad never got to see me pull on a Cardinals jersey. He was a die hard fan and would have really gotten a kick out of that."

The ironic thing was that for that afternoon anyway, Rogers could only speculate on how all that felt. He didn't remember a thing.

"Is it safe to assume that you were named after former Cardinals great, Rogers Hornsby?" a young, female reporter asked.

"Well, since Rogers Hornsby is the only other Rogers I've ever even heard about, I think that's a pretty safe assumption," he laughed.

"Prior to your arrival in St. Louis," a third reporter added, "Hornsby was considered arguably the greatest Cardinal ever. Yet, other than career batting average and triples, you've surpassed him in every other offensive category. How does that feel?"

"What do you do when you've at least statistically speaking, surpassed your father's favorite player? The guy regarded at the best in the organization's history?" Rogers asked, shaking his head. "It's a pretty surreal feeling to be honest."

"It's no secret that you've also managed to surpass his popularity off the field as well. *The Rajah* was not known for being the most cordial or well-liked by his teammates. Is that something you've always strived for?"

"Likeability?" Rogers chuckled.

"Yes."

"Well, no one wants to be the guy who gets booed off the Jumbotron when they're taking in a game. But I've been fortunate to have a supportive family and some great friends and mentors over the years. In the end, though, we all have our moments, both good and bad. It just depends when you catch us. The world would be a much different place if we were all judged solely by the worst thing we've ever done."

"Rogers. You're 134 home runs away from passing Willie Mays on the All-Time list. What are your feelings on that?"

"My feeling is that it sounds like a lot of work."

They all broke into laughter.

"To be honest, I'd rather win a 3rd World Series title," he added. "Anymore questions? No? Thanks, guys, for coming out today and for your support over the years. It means a lot."

And somewhere, higher than the puffy, cumulus clouds he seemed to scrape with the home run ball he hit out of the stadium to win game 6 of the 2011 World Series; he knew his father was smiling.

XIII.
redemption

When someone did something magnificent—saved a life, cured a disease, won the Nobel Prize for Literature—it was a surprise if it received 20 lines in the newspaper three days after the fact. But if there was a scandal of some sort, especially of a sexual nature, every major network was likely to be camped out at your door.

As soon as the news broke of Cheryl Reuben's claim of sexual harassment against her boss at Yale, Henry Whitman's phone began ringing off the hook. At one point, he could have sworn the receiver was practically being lifted from its holder from the shear volume of calls coming in at once. He decided the proper way to address it was to hold a news conference. The Board of Trustees weren't fans of the idea at first. "All publicity is good publicity" did not necessarily apply to institutions of higher learning. But after seeing the direction the media was running in, they thought it best to give them some facts instead of speculation.

"Dr. Whitman," one of the reporters began amidst dozens of flashing camera bulbs, "When were you made aware of the allegations against Don Peterson?"

"About three days ago," Henry responded.

"What was your reaction?"

"The same as yours I'm sure. I was shocked and appalled."

"Peterson claims he's innocent and the victim of someone who was upset that they were denied a raise due to poor job performance and denied vacation time due to a lack of notice."

"All I can say to that is when the allegations were brought to my attention, we acted swiftly, but thoroughly."

"Is there any truth to Peterson's claims that Cheryl Reuben dressed provocatively and was a regular on the New Haven party circuit?" the reporter pressed.

"Every dealing I had with Miss Reuben, she was professional in every manner, including dress. As for the party circuit, I'm afraid that falls outside of my area of expertise. My party days have been over for a long time," Henry responded to laughter.

"Are you concerned at how the negative publicity will affect Yale?"

"Obviously, anytime you love a place as I love Yale, you are concerned about the possibility of it being shown in a negative light, but my concern right now is for the victims in the Yale family."

"After what happened at Penn State, are you worried about your own job?" another reporter asked.

"I haven't even given that a second thought to

be honest," Henry answered.

"Dr. Whitman, what would you say to someone who blamed you for this since it happened on your watch?" a fresh-faced reporter questioned.

It was always the young reporters that were looking to make a name for themselves by throwing out the difficult questions.

Henry hesitated for a moment before answering, "I'd tell them they were right. The buck stops at the Office of the President, and since I'm the President at this university, that would be me. That's all I have time for right now, but as we get more information, we'll keep you updated."

Henry burrowed his way through the crowd to a waiting vehicle, where his wife waited inside. She ran her hand through his hair and kissed him.

"I'm so proud of you," she said.

"You shouldn't be," was Henry's response.

"Why not?"

"Because I never should have let this happen."

"You can't be in 20 places at once at all times. Your job is all encompassing. It makes for a nice sound bite to say everything stops at the office of the President, but the reality is much different."

His wife always had a way of speaking plainly and with such logic that it often made him feel silly for not seeing it that way. But guilt had a way of clouding reality.

"My 'job' is to protect my employees and I didn't do that," he said.

"You had no way of knowing what Don Peterson was really like."

"I knew he was a scumbag. I didn't know he was *this* big of a scumbag, but I knew he was one and I looked the other way. I always justified it in my mind because he was able to raise more money for the university than anyone ever had, and I thought that money could be used for research and scholarships for students who otherwise never would have had the opportunity to attend Yale. I thought the good outweighed the bad."

"I think you're being too hard on yourself."

"I don't think I'm being hard enough."

"Have you heard anything from the Board?"

"They have suggested I take an 'early retirement'. They'll give me my pension and let me go out on my own terms at the end of the year. Not that anyone will believe it."

"That doesn't seem fair."

"In my eyes, it's fair," Henry said. "And at least now I can look you and our daughter in the eyes and know I did the right thing."

"You always do the right thing."

Henry shook his head. "Not always."

His wife had no idea what he meant.

Later that evening, once the last of the reporters had left the grounds, Henry visited a small cape cod home with a neatly kept yard on the outskirts of the Yale campus. He composed himself and rang the bell. Cheryl looked frazzled and a bit surprised, but happy to see him.

"Dr. Whitman? Please come in," she said.

"Thank you, but I don't want to bother you.

And I apologize for showing up at your home unannounced like this, but I wanted you to know how sorry I am about everything that's happened. I feel responsible."

"You're the one who put a stop to it. For that, I'm extremely grateful. A lot of people wouldn't have even done that."

"Well, I wish I could have prevented it altogether."

"There's no way you could have. I should have stood up to him sooner."

"Don't even think about blaming yourself," Henry interjected. "I want you to know that no matter what, you will always have a job with me. Wherever I am."

"Am I about to lose my job??" she panicked.

"No. But it looks like I might. And I just wanted you to know that wherever I land, you're welcome to come. If you ever get tired of Yale or just want a change."

"I don't understand," she said, "Why would you lose your job?"

"The Board will probably want to make a statement by holding someone responsible. And as Don's boss, that person would be me."

"Oh my god, I feel horrible."

"You have no reason to feel horrible. I didn't come here for that. I came here for you. I'll be fine. Don't worry about me. I've been thinking about going back into teaching for a while now anyway. I'm happiest in a classroom."

Cheryl stepped outside and hugged him tightly.

She felt awful that the man who actually defended her was losing his job. He didn't feel worthy of her sympathy. Cheryl Reuben wasn't his daughter; but this could have happened to his daughter. And that's probably what bothered him most.

XIV.
an extraordinary life

Hundreds of people lined the red carpet outside the Kodak Theatre looking for a glimpse of their favorite stars. Limos extended three blocks of Hollywood Boulevard waiting to drop off their passengers. The drivers all knew each other. It was as if they had their own unspoken language. They even seemed to have their own caste system. The ones that drove the most famous stars, received the most respect. Mo's driver fell somewhere in the middle of the pecking order.

Hector was his date, and looked considerably different in a black tuxedo jacket and white shirt without a tie, than he had in his grey, polyester, short-sleeved button down car wash shirt, with his name and title sewn on in red cursive. Mo was signing autographs on the way into the theatre for woman and children only until a 40-something man thrust a piece of paper in his face.

"Seriously, dude?" Mo asked.

"It's for my wife. She's a big fan," the man replied.

Hector fired an elbow into Mo's rib section, and made no attempt whatsoever to disguise it. Mo shook his head before relenting and signing the paper.

He eventually made his way to the entrance, where he was cornered by the television tabloids.

"We're here with Tony and Academy Award winning actor, Mo Falls, who has just arrived for the premier of his latest film *An Hour After Midnight*, which also stars Robert DeNiro," the reporter stated.

Mo wondered if there was going to be a question anywhere in his future.

"Rumor has it you and DeNiro became pretty tight during the filming of this movie," the reporter continued. "What was it like working with such a Hollywood legend?"

"We actually just met about five minutes ago on the carpet over there," Mo answered. "He seems like a good guy."

As far as Mo remembered, he *had* just met him and he wasn't in the mood to play along. It had been a long couple of days. Even the normally unflappable Mo had his tipping point.

"Always the kidder! So, in this movie you play a gang leader in South Central Los Angeles who lives next door to DeNiro's character—a former mafia don who's in the witness protection program. They're calling it *Boyz in the Hood* meets *The Godfather*. What first got you interested in the script?"

"I have no idea."

The reporter laughed nervously, "But seriously..."

"Seriously, I have no idea. But I'm sure it was something. Probably the money if I had to guess."

The reporter wasn't sure what to make of Mo's responses.   He   was   growing   increasingly uncomfortable and would have been wise to cut his losses and move on to someone else. But he forged on nonetheless. "There's been a lot of buzz about this film already, and talk about the possibility of you becoming one of only 21 other actors to win two academy awards for Best Actor. What are your feelings about that?"

"Here's the thing," Mo said. "I don't see how there can be buzz about a movie no one has seen yet. If they're basing it off the pitch or storyline, and we *don't* end up winning any acting awards, then I guess that means we failed as actors."

"Umm, ah...okaaay—"

"I've got to head inside. Thanks, bro."

Mercifully, it was finally over. Mo turned to Hector once they were safely out of ear shot. "I should have used my redo opportunity to kill that guy."

"You would get no argument from me," Hector agreed.

Mo and Hector had seats in the roped off area in the middle of the theatre. It was lit somewhere between bright and dim, and the crowd was murmuring and looking around to see if anyone more famous than they were had entered the room. A man hurriedly sat down next to Mo--the film's very famous director.

"Mo. I have to say that I heard great things about you both personally and professionally before you agreed to do this film."

"You did?" Mo asked, surprised.

"And I have to say, you surpassed all my expectations," the man added.

"I did?" Mo answered, even more surprised.

"I was hoping we could sit down next week sometime to talk about future projects. I'd love to work with you again."

"You would?"

And just like that, the director was gone. Vanished like a character in one of his movies.

Mo turned to Hector for some clarity. "Who *is* this person these people are talking about?? I don't even recognize him!"

"You don't recognize the *old* Mo Falls."

"So you mean to tell me that just because I didn't spend three months in a Mexican prison, my entire life is different?"

Mo paused for a moment to reflect on that statement, before adding, "Now that I say that out loud, I can see how that might make sense."

"In addition to getting excellent career advice from your wise agent, not going to jail, meant that people on Broadway were less reluctant to give you a chance. Which in turn gave you some credibility. Which in turn enabled you to win 5 Tony Awards. Which in turn enabled you to work on some passion projects—"

"Which in turn led to my bank account shrinking from 200 million to 90 million dollars. I know. I checked today."

"I was going to say which in turn enabled you to win an Academy Award."

"And a shrinking bank account."

"No one said following your passion came cheaply."

"If my agent really was wise, he would have informed me that the cost of following my passion would be 110 million dollars, in which case, I would have done a fucking sitcom instead!"

"No one forced your hand. We each control our own destiny," Hector said simply.

A woman slid into the seat next to him. *Stunning*. Familiar looking. She kissed Mo on the lips.

"I'm sorry I'm late, babe. Rehearsal ran long and then we had to fight a horrific head wind the whole way from New York," she said.

Mo turned back to Hector and whispered, "I'm dating Alicia Keys??!!"

"It would appear so," Hector answered, tipping his glasses down for a better look.

"Oh, man. Swizz Beat is gonna be peeiisssed!"

XV.
a lesson well learned

Katy Conner was as beautiful as you might expect from the wife of a world class athlete. She was tall, blonde, and confident, with equal doses of sharp business woman crossed with Head of the PTA. She knew *of* Rogers when they were both at Choate, although they never met until a chance encounter a few months into the year.

He was the star athlete. She ran with the theatre crowd, spending her free time acting in plays when she wasn't studying. Katy was playing Belle in Choate's joint production of *Beauty and the Beast* with the O'Neil Center Theatre group when Rogers walked in with Matt O'Malley and their two dates. To say Rogers was mesmerized was an understatement. He couldn't describe it without sounding foolish, but there was something beyond her looks, something about the inflection of her voice when she spoke, something about the sparkle in her eyes when she looked at him that captured his heart fully.

Matt managed to get them all invited to the cast party following the show and even though Rogers feigned interest in his date, she knew his real interest was elsewhere and asked to go home. Matt, in the way only the best of friends could, convinced his date to stay in order to give Rogers a reason to return and pick them up.

Rogers made the hour and twenty minute round trip in forty-seven minutes. It left him with just enough time to ask Katy to dance and convince her he wasn't some Neanderthal. When she left that night, she remained unconvinced, and it took three more *"chance"* encounters before she agreed to go on a date with him.

With money very much an object, Rogers needed to be creative. He opted for pumpkin picking at a local farm that doubled as a haunted farm for Halloween, followed by hot apple cider on the patio. It wasn't at all what she expected. They began dating shortly thereafter, but called it off after graduation due to the distance between Brown, where she went, and Notre Dame. They dated other people for the first two years of college before coming to the simultaneous realization that they were both perfect for each other. She came from family money—her father had been the CEO at Motorola-- so Rogers didn't have to worry that she was only with him for an eventual big payday. And following the 2000 Olympics, Rogers had become more famous than she was, even after her supporting role in an independent film landed her on Entertainment Weekly's *It List*.

They were engaged two years after graduation, and shared a small apartment in Manhattan. While he was toiling around the Cardinals farm system with stops in Peoria, New Haven and Memphis, she was starring on Broadway alongside a reformed and burgeoningly popular, Mo Falls—who had introduced them at the O'Neill School.

Six months after Rogers signed his first big league contract, they were married in an elaborate ceremony in the Chicago suburb where her family lived. They had a cute, tomboy of a daughter who was now ten, and a yellow lab that moped around the more than 10,000 square foot house they lived in looking for his master, whenever Rogers was traveling with the team.

And yet, despite all of their shared history, his wife was little more than a stranger he had met for the first time fours hours ago. It was a strange and yet exciting feeling at the same time. As if he was getting to experience falling in love all over again.

"Have you spoken to Sam recently?" Rogers asked that afternoon.

"As in your sister?"

"Yes."

"She's out of the country this week."

"Which would explain why her phone went straight to voicemail when I called," Rogers replied.

"Can you pick up Sheri from soccer practice at 6:30?"

"Sheri being our daughter?"

"Unless you know of a different Sheri."

"Sure. Where are they practicing?"

Katy furrowed her brow.

"Wolfe Park? Same place you've picked her

up a thousand times."

"Just making sure," Rogers stammered. Although his father had brought him back to visit St. Louis several times when he was a kid, he really didn't know his way around. He would have to figure this one out on his own.

"And no stopping off at the Go Carts and Bumper Boats on the way home," Katy smiled. "Matt and Carla will be here for dinner any minute."

"Matt as in O'Malley?" Rogers asked hopefully. He had never wanted to see someone so much in his life. In the muddled world that was now his, he wanted someone to share in the confusion.

"As in Ward. Your teammate for the last seven years. Are you ok?" she asked. "You seem kind of out of it today."

"Just tired from traveling."

"And can you do me a favor tonight?"

"What's that?"

"Try to talk some sense into Matt. Carla's going to leave him if he doesn't commit to her soon."

"Commit as in get married?"

"Of course."

"He's young, successful and rich. Why would he want to do that?" Rogers reasoned.

"Because he won't always be. He might be rich, but he won't be young forever and he doesn't want to end up a sad, solo ex-athlete whose daily highlight is watching Sports Center and telling tales to no one about how great he once was."

"Is that what you saw for my future before you married me?" Rogers laughed. It wasn't far off.

"Precisely. But at least you were smart enough to marry a wonderful wife."

The doorbell rang and Katy made her way down a long corridor that opened into a raised entry way. The wooden doors had to be 15 feet high. She gave it a good tug just to open it. Standing on the front step was Rogers teammate, Matt Ward, and his girlfriend of seven years. Katy kissed them both on the cheek. Rogers kissed Carla and then brought Matt in for a handshake and shoulder bump. He actually knew Matt in his previous life and had always liked him, having played in a couple of All Star games together. It made sense now that they were on the same team, that they were friends. Matt was blonde, with movie star, well-chiseled features. He had been a regular fixture in Sports Illustrated's *Body Issue* over the years. Carla was some sort of Spanish, with the unusual combination of blue eyes and dark hair, with full beautiful lips and the body of a fitness instructor. She was actually a pediatric physician.

"Are you boys ready for opening day tomorrow? Going to kick some Cubbie ass?" Katy asked.

"You better believe it. Going to be an exciting day with the President coming to town," Matt answered.

"The President's coming?" Rogers asked.

"Uh, yeah. Where have you been?"

"I haven't been paying very close attention obviously," Rogers laughed. "Hey, let's take a ride. I have to go pick Sheri up at Wolfe Park."

"Lead the way. I always get lost in this Disneyworld of homes. Can we take the Carrera?" Matt asked.

"That's a good question. Can we?" Rogers asked his wife.

She looked a little uncertain.

"Wolfe Park is only ten minutes from here," Matt offered. "And technically, it does have a back seat.

When Katy didn't say *no*, Rogers took it as a *yes*. He started down the hallway. The wrong hallway.

"The car's parked in the garage, not the bedroom," Katy pointed out before turning to Carla, "He's been like this all day. You better get to bed early tonight."

Rogers inserted the key into the opening on the left of the steering wheel, as was the case on all Porsche's and turned it. The car sounded like a rocket engine just prior to take off.

"Why do Porsches have the ignition on the left?" Matt asked.

"Because in the old days, race car drivers used to go from a running start and jump into their cars. Having the ignition on the left gave them a split second advantage," Rogers explained.

"No kidding. So how much did this bad boy set you back?"

"I don't really know to be honest."

"Must be nice to be so rich you don't even ask how much something costs. You just buy it," Matt laughed.

"I don't think you're worrying about where your next meal is coming from."

"That's because I know where it's coming from. Your wife is cooking it! You think she could teach Carla how to cook?"

"That depends. When are you going to make an honest woman out of Carla?" Rogers transitioned.

"You mean, ask her to marry me?"

"That would be the next logical step."

"When I absolutely have to," was Matt's frank response.

"Why not? She's smart, sweet, beautiful."

"I'm young, a celebrity and rich. Why the hell would I want to do that?"

He did have a point.

"Because you're not always going to be," Rogers tried.

"Why are you trying to shoot holes in my plan?"

"Listen, I get it. Going to clubs where people buy you drinks and food even though you make ten times what they make. Girls throwing themselves at you in every city we play in. Going out on the party train where you just need to point and you can bang four chicks in a night. Having girls offer to blow you under the table of a crowded night club."

"I don't know what the hell party train you were on, but I definitely want to get on that," Matt said.

"I know it all seems great now, but trust me, you don't want to be that guy on the downside of his career, getting booed off the Jumbotron at an NBA game because everyone thinks he's a selfish asshole, banging some hooker in an executive suite because you're starving for attention of some kind."

"What would you know about any of that? You married your high school sweetheart when you were 24."

"I know more than you think. Jack Hughes used to tell me about it when I first came up to the bigs."

"No kidding. What's he doing these days?"

"Living in Vegas, signing autographs at memorabilia shows, gambling by day, and clubbing all night with people he doesn't even know because all of his friends are married."

"That's.....kind of sad."

"That could be you, my man, if the price is right."

"That won't be me," Matt assured him.

"I sure hope not. But let me ask you something. Do you love her?"

"Of course I do."

"Then this is all I'll say and I promise to drop it after," Rogers said. "Don't trade 50 years of happiness for the next five."

XVI.
a life replaced

The sound of Katy's snoring was only amplified by the fact that Rogers couldn't sleep. He laid staring at the ceiling in a room lit only by subtle moonlighting. His mind was racing between memories from a previous life, and a concern over his current one. When he was unable to take it any longer, he slid out from beneath the covers, grabbed his cell phone from the nightstand next to the bed, and went downstairs.

Rogers removed a small piece of paper from the pocket of a jacket that hung on a chair in the living room and punched in the number on his phone. He seemed surprised when the word "Mo" appeared on his phone screen after he had entered the last number.

"What's up Big Man?" the voice on the other end of the line asked.

"How'd you know it was me?" Rogers asked.

"Because your name popped up. Apparently, we're friends in this life."

"Did I wake you?"

"It's only ten o'clock in California, bro."

"Right. Well, I can't sleep. Or maybe I just don't want to sleep."

"What's the problem?"

"The guy said after we go to sleep the first night, when we wake up in the morning, it will be as if our previous life never happened. We won't remember any of it."

"And how's your new life?"

"It's different."

"Different bad or different good?"

"Different good for the most part. I play for the Cardinals. Married a girl I met during my PG year at Choate—"

"I know. I introduced the two of you. You and O'Malley came over to see a play I was in at the O'Neill Center in Connecticut. You each had dates, but you couldn't take your eyes off my co-star."

"How do you know all that?"

"Hector told me."

"How does Hector know all that?"

"Hector is a Google whore."

There were loud musical noises in the background at Mo's. Someone was playing the piano. And singing.

Although it was slightly muffled, Rogers recognized the voice and the song.

"Are you at a club?" he asked.

"Nah, man. I'm having a little gathering at my house following my movie premier," Mo answered.

"You're in a movie?"

"Yes, sir."

"Is it any good?"

"I was exceptional, if I do say so myself."

"Who's playing the piano and singing in the background? They're *really* good."

"That would be my girlfriend."

"She does a spot on cover of Alicia Keys," Rogers said.

"She should. She *is* Alicia Keys.

Rogers could almost *see* Mo's smirk through the phone.

"Get the hell out."

"Truth," Mo smiled.

"Wow. Sounds like your life turned out all right."

"It turned out differently than I expected, but I just roll with things, baby. You should do the same."

"I'm just worried I'm going to forget certain memories and people that I don't want to forget," Rogers explained.

"Well, you won't forget me."

"Not sure whether that's good or bad," Rogers answered. "Have you spoken to O'Malley? His number is in my phone, so I'm assuming we're friends, but when I called, it went straight to voice mail."

"Well, he's probably pretty busy."

"What makes you say that?"

"Did you happen to watch the news, read a paper, surf the internet or listen to the radio today?" Mo asked.

"I was traveling most of the day. Why?"

"No reason."

"Nevermind. He's calling me right now."

"Go ahead and take it, so I can get back to my party. I'll see you at Opening Day tomorrow."

"You're coming?"

"It's on my calendar, so apparently yes."

"See ya then," Rogers said before he clicked over. "Matt."

"Hey. Sorry it took me a while to get back to you," was the response. "It's been kind of a hectic day."

"Good hectic or bad hectic?"

"A little of both actually."

"Your life turn out the way you hoped?"

"You could say that. I ended up going to the prom with this cute girl who asked me that I blew off the first time, and we ended up getting married. She's the heiress to the Grey Poupon mustard fortune."

"Just as easy to fall in love with a rich girl as it is a poor one."

"That's true. It does make some things easier. I see you're playing for the Cardinals."

"Yup. My dad would have loved it."

"And got married."

"To some girl Mo apparently introduced me to. Not sure how I feel about that."

"About Mo introducing you or getting married?"

"Not sure how I feel about anyone who was friends with Mo Falls," Rogers laughed. "Are you nervous about waking up tomorrow and forgetting things that happened?"

"A little. But then I think this is how things

were meant to be if we hadn't screwed it up the first time."

"I guess."

"Look, I've got to go. But I'll see you at your game."

"You're coming too?"

"Everyone's coming. Including your sister," Matt said.

"How do you know my sister's coming? Please tell me you're not sleeping with her."

"I promise you I'm not. Didn't you watch the news today at all?"

"Why does everyone keep asking me that? I was traveling."

"Well, if you had, you'd know that your sister was the Secretary of State," Matt said.

"For which state??" Rogers asked.

"She's *the* Secretary of State. For the United States."

"Are you joking?"

"I guess you were right when you told Dr. Whitman that she would one day wind up being one of the most distinguished alums in Choate history. But I've got to run," Matt said. "I'll see you tomorrow."

Rogers went back upstairs and climbed into bed next to his snoring wife. In less than six hours, a host of memories would be forever lost, as if they were a part of a dream he couldn't quite remember. He finally drifted off to sleep, his old life behind him, and his new one, set to officially begin.

XVII.
opening day

Long before he ever held a bat in his hands, Rogers had loved opening day. They had a tradition where his father would take him to St. Louis, and they would watch the Cardinals with most of his extended family that lived there. Fathers and sons. Families smiling and laughing together. It was Christmas in early April, with the sun managing to scare away the last remnants of winter. Vendors weren't just selling hot dogs, peanuts and cracker jacks. They were selling hope. Every team was undefeated on opening day, and every team had a chance, before the bad bounces, injuries and dog days of summer, derailed their dreams.

As a player, the occasional whiff of a hot dog was drowned out by the indescribable smell of freshly cut grass whose morning dew had just melted away.

As a fan, stadiums had always looked enormous, and players seemed as though they were in a different zip code from them. And yet, from the field, he could clearly spot and describe a person in the upper deck. He also now noticed something he had never had paid much attention to before; how every little boy's face lit up when he tossed them a ball, signed their program, or even spoke a kind word to them.

Rogers strode to the batter's box for batting practice and pointed to one of the luxury suites behind home plate. He waved to his family and friends. They were all there. His wife, daughter, sister, mother, Mo, Jimmy, Hector—even Henry Whitman. They were enjoying themselves, this group of new old friends. But there was no sign of Matt O'Malley.

After putting on a display that saw him launch five or six balls deep into the seats to the delight of the crowd, he headed back to the clubhouse to pull on his freshly pressed #17 jersey. No matter how many times he had done it before, it was a feeling that would never get old.

The Cardinals catcher, Teddy Haley, handed him his glove.

"Here you go, big man. Dissed by the President. I can't believe he asked for our 1st baseman to catch the Ceremonial First Pitch," he said, only half joking.

"What can I say? I'm a living legend," Rogers joked.

"Yeah yeah."

"The President must love the long ball. Anything special I need to know about trying to catch a baseball with this oven mitt?"

"Yeah. Open it up before the ball arrives, and close it after it does."

"Gee, thanks for the advice."

"No problem," Haley smirked as the public address announcer began in the background.

"Ladies and gentlemen," the announcer began. "Please direct your attention to the field where Cardinals 1st baseman, Rogers Conner, will catch today's special ceremonial first pitch."

The crowd roared. It was an ovation suitable for a living legend. Even he seemed a bit surprised by both its' loudness and duration. Rogers tipped his cap. Twice.

"And now...making his way to the mound on opening day 2014 is a very special guest indeed. Please rise and welcome our Commander-in-Chief, the 45th President of the United States, MATTHEW A. O'MALLEY!!!!"

The crowd roared again. Not quite as loudly as for Rogers, because after all, it was St. Louis. Matt, sporting a nylon, navy Cardinals pitcher's jacket with red and white writing, stepped onto the mound like a veteran.

He shook off the first sign from Rogers, playing to the crowd, then nodded, wheeled, and delivered a strike.

The two men met halfway between the mound and home plate for a shoulder hug.

"Thanks for coming," Rogers said, as he handed him the ball.

"Wouldn't have missed it. Although the Nats organization was sure pissed. Hit one out for me, will ya?"

"I'll do my best."

"By the way," Matt said, "You were correct when you told Dr. Whitman that your sister would end up being one of the most distinguished graduates Choate ever had. Just not *the* most distinguished," he added with a wink.

On the walkway just above the field boxes behind the home dugout, two men were speaking. One was sporting a Cardinals cap with a short-sleeved button down shirt and khaki pants. The other had a #17 Cardinals jersey on over an Oxford shirt and jeans. It was difficult to pinpoint why, but they looked a bit out of place. A closer look revealed two of the Knights of Redemption. The one in the cap was the one who had spoken to Matt.

"Section 121. We've got the guy pretty agitated. I think he'll be starting a fight any minute now," the one in the jersey said.

"Just make sure no one gets hurt in the process," the other man answered.

"Security is already over there and have been paid appropriately to handle it."

Rogers stepped into the on deck circle and eyed the men. They looked familiar, but he couldn't place them.

"What about the others?" the man in the cap continued.

"Two of them are in jail already. Picked up one for DUI. Another for shoplifting. Still working on the other two."

"Now batting for the Cardinals. The 1st Baseman. Number 17. Rogers. Conner," the PA announcer droned.

"Plant some coke in the guy's locker at his country club, and send over a hooker to nab the 5th one. We don't have all day. It's not like anyone will ever remember any of it anyway."

"You got it, boss," the man in the jersey said. He started to walk away, then stopped and turned around. "Can you imagine how different the world would be if everyone was judged solely by the worst mistake they ever made?"

The other man smiled. "That's where we come in, my friend. Keep me posted."

And then—*SMACK!* The sellout crowd leapt to its collective feet as Rogers smashed the first pitch thrown to him somewhere toward the St. Louis Arch. Some ballplayers had short, compact, explosive swings, but Rogers had a long, smooth, loping, pure swing that when he made contact with a ball, sent it soaring into the sky. This ball continued its ascent to the point where it seemed to disappear into the clouds for an instant, before beginning its descent and landing deep into the center field bleachers.

A crowd of people, adults and children alike, scurried to find the ball, until a boy of about seven thrust his arm into the air triumphantly, gripping the white leather ball with the red stitching tightly in the palm of his hand as Rogers rounded third base and headed for home.

XVIII.
epilogue

It all started from an overheard conversation at a bar. One of the Knights listened as Matt O'Malley told a bartender about the "one that got away" and how his life would be much different if he hadn't let it happen. After weeks of research and observation, they came to realize that five men from completely different walks of life, not only had more in common that it appeared at first glance, but they also each had the ability to help one of the others.

So the Knights set a plan into action, first hiring a prostitute to seduce Rogers at the Knicks game. That was an easy one. They then hired a mechanic to deem Mo's plane unfit to fly and plant drugs in his luggage prior to turning it over to the airlines. They had pictures of Matt's wife with his campaign manager at a hotel that were set to go out with the morning mail, when fate intervened in the form of his wife's accident. They didn't need to send the envelope after all. For months, Hector had been trying to find a way to get his daughter out of the school system she was in. He only needed someone to give him the idea how to do it and assure him there was nothing terribly wrong with it. As for Dr.

Henry Whitman? The one person who had never made a wrong decision in his life, made one at the exact moment they needed him to. A "janitor" that had discreetly followed Henry's every move, was there when he did. The Knights did, however, have a contingency plan lined up just in case Henry had stayed the course.

Of course, they had no way of knowing how it would all turn out, but once they were done, they agreed it had been, by far, the most successful project to date. Matt went on to become the most popular and successful President in recent history. Rogers and Mo used their fame and fortune to help thousands of people with charity work. Katy and Hector were the people behind the people, that had helped shape Rogers and Mo into the people they had become. And Henry was the centerpiece that held the entire puzzle together.

From there, the Knights moved onto their next project, using money from one of the most prestigious universities in the country, from an endowment funded by some of the wealthiest people in the world. In essence, it was people helping people, even if many of the ones helping, knew nothing about it.

Although there were only five "Knights", they now had literally thousands of helpers, "Squires" if you will, and the goal was to work hard enough that they could eventually work themselves right out of a job. They wanted earth to become a mere stepping-stone to heaven, knowing full well making that happen would be nearly impossible. But they pressed on anyway.....leading men, women and children alike down a path that most of them didn't even realize they were on—the path to redemption.

Acknowledgments

First and foremost, I would like to thank my "editing" crew past and present: PJ O'Leary, Dan Holmes, Steve Abbott, Sara Marangola, and Zac Shaw. All of you went beyond the call of friendship by reading my stories over and over again until I got it right (assuming I did), when I'm sure you had better things to do.

For those of you whose names appear in this book, you are great friends with great sounding names. You may not be famous, but your name is now in print for all of eternity.

To my parents, who always encouraged me to express myself by writing and were supportive in every way possible, I hope ebooks are available in heaven, and my apologies for my occasional "colorful" language in this story.

Finally, to my wife, Katy, who had to endure endless pitch sessions, and constant questions about whether a story or character "worked", thank you from the bottom of my heart for your encouragement and inspiration.

MATT MICROS received a B.A. in American Studies from the University of Notre Dame and his M.S. in Television, Radio and Film from Syracuse's Newhouse School of Communications, before spending seven years in Los Angeles working in television production, followed by a stint at Creative Artists Agency. He currently resides in Stratford, Connecticut with his wife, Katy, and their dog, Mr. Beans.